Their Souls

Met in

Wishton

Wanda Penalver Bevan

Dedication

For Maurine

*"Believe me when I say
I need you like oxygen*

*Believe the soul in you
that's found the soul in me
and will not let go because
it needs the other to thrive*

*Close your eyes and
watch the painting unfold
Onto the canvas of my heart"*

WPB

Prologue

A little girl and a little boy stood next to a beautiful waterfall.

"What's that you're holding?" the little boy asked.

"It's my heart," the little girl said.

"May I have it?" he asked her.

"Yes, you may," the little girl replied, and gave her heart to him.

"May I have yours?" asked the little girl.

"Yes, you may," he said to her and handed her his heart.

The little girl pointed to the rainbow that appeared above the waterfall and said, "We have many waterfalls to walk beneath and many rivers to cross, many things to embrace and discover and many appointments to keep."

"What if we become parted as we encounter all these things?" he asked.

"Part, we must," she answered.

"But why?" the little boy asked.

"Because the destiny chosen for you and me is to grow and learn, hurt and heal, give and receive, and travel our intended paths. At the time we are supposed to, we will find each other again," she said.

"But how can you be sure?" asked the boy.

He watched as the girl disappeared through the waterfall and heard her say from the other side, "Because nothing can keep you from finding the one who holds your heart."

Chapter One

Take The Long Way Home
Supertramp, 1979

"Now, that's a book I would read."

The statement traveled from the other side of the neutral toned, shabby-chic decorated living room, followed by a few lukewarm affirmatives. Being terrible with names, I decided to identify the gregarious, earth-mother type as simply Member No. 8.

I wasn't even sure why I was here. Now that Sean and Cassandra were in high school, everyone kept telling me it's time to take up some former hobbies I've been putting on the backburner over the years. When a friend of mine told me about the book club that met on Wednesday night in Sherman Oaks, I thought it might be just the nudge I needed to get started—on those backburner hobbies, that is. I hadn't finished reading a book since I'd brought my newborn babies home from the hospital, and I've even taken the first step by making a list of goals to set for myself. Making a list of goals was what I'd taught my kids to do, so the same should apply to me, I thought.

Decide/Do a professor in college had written once in a critique of my work. *Less thinking, more doing*, he had said. I framed the note and hung it in every house I lived in since I was twenty-one. Though I have yet to master the Decide/Do formula, it always made perfect sense to me that Decide was probably married to Goal, and together, they gave birth to Do. What worried me was whether the item I'd put at the top of my very carefully thought-out list might take the rest of my life to complete: *Figuring Out My Life's Purpose.*

"You mean a collection of love letters by Keats—a nineteenth century tortured soul—to the woman he loved?" Member No. 7 asked as she pushed her Kate Spade eyeglasses back in their position on the bridge of her nose. It reminded me how important it is to have a well-fitting pair of glasses, and that I've always found it interesting how clothing designers always end up having their name on multitudes of things that aren't clothes. "Or anything and everything scribbled onto a napkin by one of the Brontë sisters?"

The Brontë sisters. Just the sound of the phrase rekindled my hope that if reincarnation is real, please let me return as one of them.

"No, I mean something about someone in this day and time who experienced something like that," explained 8. "A modern story about two people who have always been deeply connected, you know? Maybe life circumstances drove them apart, but then brought them back together, and nothing can keep them apart, you know? My God, she says at one point, 'I *am* Heathcliff.'"

"Best line in the book, if ya ask me," No. 2 chimed in, punctuating the remark with the crunch of a pita chip smothered in garlic hummus.

"Oh, definitely, the best line," agreed No. 4, with more authority than admiration, leaving me to speculate if somewhere in her profile was the background of an educator whose area of expertise was classic literature, or just being a know-it-all.

My vote was for Wuthering Heights, though for the moment, I kept it to myself. For as far back as I could remember, I'd been captivated by the story of Cathy and Heathcliff and every Hollywood movie version of it—even the bad ones. I idolized the Brontë sisters, which was probably partly attributed to being raised by an English teacher. Classic literature and correct grammar were fed to me from the time I could chew solid food. Even now, I still can't decide which would be more fabulous, to be an actress who has the opportunity to play Catherine Earnshaw, or be the author that created her.

"But theirs was not exactly a healthy relationship," No. 3 pointed out with a smirk. She certainly got that right. But it wasn't clear if the chiseled frown in her leathery forehead indicated a dislike for the melodramatic or years of too much fun in the sun.

"Healthy relationships don't make the best dramatic literature," 2 replied.

"So true!" was the response from over half the group. I nodded my head in agreement, hoping no one would notice my imagination drifting off to the Moors of England where Catherine Earnshaw called her home.

No. 5 seemed to almost channel the spirit of John Keats, the poet in question, speaking in a melodious but barely audible whisper that forced everyone in the room to lean towards her. "Well, I vote for Keats. He was a genius and his love for Fanny Braun was like his love affair with everything else he found beautiful in life. The true, bleeding poet—"

"—who'd rather die than be without the thing that's killing him, anyway," No. 9 snapped.

The comment made me think of the hundreds of poems I'd written in my lifetime and if anything would ever become of them. If not, it was okay, because they'd served their purpose in the instant they spilled onto the paper. Once purged, a healing always occurred. It was a soothing recovery that refilled the well for me to pour out more the next time. I would love to have known Keats.

"So sad. Poor guy was only twenty-five when he died," No. 6 pointed out, who didn't appear to be much older than twenty-five herself. I was dying to know the meaning behind the sinister looking tattoo splattered in all directions about her neck, and was determined to ask her before she left tonight. I'll word it in a polite, friendly, if-you-don't-mind-my-asking sort of way, instead of what I'd really like to say, which is, "Excuse me, that thing resembling a wall mural you're walking around with is so interesting, you must get this question all the time. What's it mean?" Of course, I could just keep my mouth shut, but my curiosity is far too piqued.

No. 4 looked up from her iPhone. "You gotta remember, folks didn't live long back then. Once your sore throat turned into something else, your days were numbered."

The person who spoke next was Sheila, the woman whose house this was and who put the group together. Thank goodness I'd remembered her name, at least.

"Well, as much as I'm sure none of us would mind reading Wuthering Heights for, what, the tenth time?—maybe we should give old Mr. Keats a shot. But it's poetry, folks. Can everybody hang with that? And it's really, really, heavy-handed language. Do you want to start with the letters to Fanny Braun?"

"If we have to," teased 8.

"Well, we did say at the last meeting that the next couple picks would be from the classics. And what I think we'll find interesting about John Keats is, here is this man, barely a full grown man, almost a boy, who spilled out all this amazing poetry," Sheila continued. "I mean listen to this, 'I almost wish we were butterflies and lived but three summer days. Three such days with you I could fill with more delight than fifty common years could ever contain.'"

"Mmm. So beautiful," sighed 5.

"*And* he was studying to be a doctor, so he was a catch," Sheila went on. A round of laughter floated within the soothing, sand-colored walls beneath the home's high ceilings.

"Talk about conflicted," 3 added, producing a second round of laughs.

It didn't seem odd to me at all that Keats walked the artist vs. pragmatist line during his short life. I'd suffered the same malady for many years myself and doubted I was the only one in the room who had. The eternal tug of war between the creative me and the business me, always struggling to win the other over, pulling the other over to their side, convinced the grass was greener there, and that the only sure way to succeed in life was to choose one or the other.

Decide/Do.

Keats had done that much, at least. Emily Brontë had done the same. That's what life was about. With every birthday, it was becoming clearer to me that it didn't matter whether your pool was a clear, chlorinated, crystal blue, or a yummy vat of chocolate. All that mattered was that you jumped into it with all fours.

For the first time in the evening, I felt motivated to speak.

"You know the thing about him that intrigues me the most?"

"Oh, everybody, this is Miranda," Sheila interjected. "She's joining us for the first time tonight so please welcome her. And you're a writer, correct?"

I forced a grin and replied modestly, "Um, not sure."

I wasn't trying to be coy. It was the truth. I really wasn't sure. Buried in the bottom of my grandmother's beautiful, hand-carved cedar chest—of the handful of precious family heirlooms in our home, it was my favorite—were poems and stories I'd written that my mother had saved since I was six years old. Though I'd changed careers more than three times since college, writing seemed to be the one constant throughout my life. Unfortunately, I'd just read an article with the sobering title, *Writing is an Art, Publishing is a Business.* There it was again, that frustrating dichotomy. And I knew I could never like the latter. I didn't even know if I was any good at the former.

"'You can, you should, and if you're brave enough to start, you will.' Stephen King," said 8, shooting a wink in my direction, as if she'd heard my private thoughts.

"What struck you most about Keats?" asked Sheila.

I cleared my throat a little. "How lucky we are that his greatest fear never came true."

"Which was?" 3 asked, without looking up.

My answer would sound as if it came from some far off place where, I confess, I frequently liked to dwell, but it felt fresh and immediate and affirming when it came out of my mouth. "Dying in obscurity."

My so-called profundity elicited no immediate response from the group. That's not a bad thing, I thought. It meant whoever was listening was thinking about it, that what I said had some value. After a few seconds, there were a couple thoughtful nods and some audible *wows*. I wondered if now that the new girl sounded like 'Debby Downer,' they might not want me back. But what the hell, this was southern California. Los Angeles, to be exact. There was no lack of diverse types spouting their opinions, and more than enough creative individuals who loved hearing themselves talk while clawing for a space in line to get to someone who'd listen. Who cared if I shifted the discussion? All I cared about was the exhilaration rising inside me that sent me heading for the door to get home and write.

Decide/Do.

I was going to give Number 8 her story.

Chapter Two

A Thousand Years
Sting, 1999

I couldn't believe I'd found my old high school friend, Liam Kincaid. I'd fallen madly in love with him the moment we met when I was 16. In the one and a half years he floated in and out of my life, I was never the same. His father was a Canadian aeronautics expert who was in town on an invitation from the university. When his dad's visiting professorship was over, their family left our quiet little town of Wishton and moved back to Canada. But there is no word I can think of in the English language other than cruel to describe fate's decision to have Liam Kincaid move away, leaving me behind. My memories of him now were still so warm and wonderful; certainly no one could blame me for fantasizing about what life might have been like if we'd never gone separate ways. And I'd thought about nothing else since seeing his face on Friendcenter a month ago.

There were guys that got away and, whether you realized it or not, you were probably damn lucky that they did. Then, there's the one that got away that leaves you with a regret you'll feel forever. Liam Kincaid was that guy for me. But no amount of thinking changes the past. No amount of wishing can turn back the clock. Yet for days my 'What Was' inventory with regard to Liam was developing into 'What Ifs.' Oh, what a love story ours might have been. And I was just the person to write it.

I was nervous about telling Liam my book idea. Though I hoped he'd be excited, or, at the very least, intrigued, I really had no idea how he'd react. Surely, he'd think it was no less than cool. Why wouldn't he? Our recent conversations confirmed he was still all the things I'd remembered him to be in high school, smart, witty, creative, with a passion for music. Of course, writing a love story about the two of us meant there would be feelings for him I'd have to reveal. I felt a dull twinge in my stomach whenever I thought about that part. That kind of disclosure would require trust. After thirty years, could I trust the man I barely knew, the way I had trusted the boy he used to be?

***

My eyes popped open in the darkness. The only thing I could see were the red digits on the alarm clock, 3:06 AM. It was the third night of sleeplessness because the ideas for the book were coming fast and furious like runaway trains. The concept sounded rather ordinary at first—a romance novel about a romance that never happened. Weren't all romance novels about romances that never happened? Unless they were non-fiction? The premise was not an unusual one; a man and woman reconnect on social media after not seeing each other for decades. As childhood friends do, they give each other a brief update of the past years—the spouses, the kids, the pets, the careers, and create a newfound friendship across the miles. That's exactly how it all started, if you started from a month ago. That's how Liam Kincaid drifted back into my unfulfilled, purpose pondering, self-searching, married—with two children—life. But the story of Liam and Miranda began a long time ago. And that's where I wanted to start.

I pounced out of bed and stumbled in the dark to our cluttered home office adjacent to the bedroom. Neil and I agreed I couldn't die first because I was the one who knew where all the important documents were. I also knew, after twenty years of marriage, that Neil could sleep through anything, so I was fairly confident I wouldn't wake him up. The sad thing was that our entire relationship had also been asleep over the past few years and there were no encouraging signs of breathing life back into it. I groped in the dark for the desk lamp and turned on the light, sending a stack of bills and Bed, Bath and Beyond coupons cascading to the floor. I clicked onto a blank white page. My fingers raced across the keyboard to catch up with the scene that was taking place in my head.

***

It was a winter's day in 1973 in a small town in upstate New York. They were in high school and secretly in love with one another. Wait—I wanted to change their names. Their names should be gentle but strong, appealing but believable, just like their characters, and not stray too far from mine and Liam's. Melinda? Monica? No. Leonard? No. Melissa and Luke? Maybe.

Shhh… Let them tell you their names, said a voice.

I breathed deeply and closed my eyes.

My two young characters introduced themselves to their author. I felt my arms wrap around them and hold them close, the way I did my children. I wasn't sure what was about to happen in their lives, but I knew I would love both of them forever.

Chapter Three

Traveling Boy
Art Garfunkel, 1970

Nicole could feel the chilly fragments of snow dropping down inside her boots as she ran as fast as she could after Garrett. Her giddy squeals only made her more out of breath while he scooped up another mound of snow and sculpted it into a perfect ball. So unfair of boys, she thought. They could always outrun her. Even if she could make a snowball as perfect as Garrett could, he would be able to out-throw her, too, just like every other boy, and some of the girls, in the eleventh grade. The one thing she would never be was an athlete. Garrett drew back his arm and pitched the snowball through the air, right for the middle of Nicole's forehead.

"Ahhh!" she roared. "No fair!"

"You're giving up," he said.

Nicole went silent. Garrett walked towards her with concern. This was her chance, she thought! To get a better aim, she needed him closer. To get him closer, she would fake being upset, as if something was wrong.

"Are you all right?" Garrett asked, trudging her way.

Nicole waited until there were only six feet between them, bent down and grabbed an enormous mound of snow, and charged towards him. Garrett took off running. Nicole caught up and hopped onto him piggy-back, mashing the cold white stuff into his face with one hand while she hung onto his neck with the other.

"Ouch—wait!" he cried.

Nicole slipped off his shoulders. Garrett's palm covered his left eye.

"Oh my God, are you okay?" she asked.

"Ahhh—I don't know. You got my eye."

Nicole panicked. They were miles from any kind of place that could deal with an emergency. She reached for his face. "Let me look—"

"No, don't touch it!" Garrett shouted, and crouched down on the ground in pain.

"Oh my God, I'm sorry! I didn't mean it."

Nicole knelt beside him in the snow, nearly in tears. Garrett started to chuckle. The chuckle turned into a laugh. The laugh became uncontrollable. He had gotten her. Again. She punched him hard on the arm.

"You are so full of it!" she said. "Why do you always do that?"

"Why are you so gullible?" He stood up and helped her onto her feet. "C'mon, we gotta get back. I don't want your mom pissed off at me."

"She would never be pissed off at you. She adores you," Nicole said.

"That's because she doesn't teach me. If she had me in class, I'd drive her nuts. Lucky for her I've got Mrs. Sherman for English instead."

They started the short trek down the hill towards his car, the firm layer of a day's worth of fallen snow crunching beneath their boots. Garrett grabbed the sleeve of Nicole's parka, pulling her to a gentle halt. With his other hand he pointed to the frosty orange horizon that rested above the Finger Lakes this time of year.

"Look at the sunset… Cool, eh?"

The view made her heart skip a beat. But then, her heart rarely beat normally when Garrett was around.

"Yeah," she whispered.

He was standing closer to her than she remembered him to be a moment ago. Still holding onto her sleeve, he trembled slightly as he leaned his face into hers, bringing them nose to nose. His nose was cold and it gave her a pleasant tingle, but when his lips parted slightly and touched hers, the heat of his breath was like intense sunshine. Her lips were soft, and the sensation shot through his veins like an injection of warm honey. A handful of snowflakes descended softly on their closed eyelids as the ground beneath them fell away, and for a few seconds they both forgot where they were. They had each dreamed about what it would be like to kiss the other, and now neither of them could believe it was happening. She would always remember the first time he kissed her, and it would join their hearts together in a way she would never be able to comprehend.

***

Garrett, Curtis, Diane and Nicole were all best friends. Nicole was a year younger than the other three, but she fell into the little group as naturally as breathing. They were all extremely bright kids who made extremely good grades and told extremely funny jokes, and although Nicole didn't share the group's obsession with Monty Python, the Three Musketeers and Doreen Greenberger, whose Harvard-bound brains and beyond perfect beauty made her the envy of all the girls and the subject of every Wishton High School boy's wet dream, it was the four of them against the post-Vietnam era of Peace and Love. Nicole regretted that she'd been born slightly later than the passionate babies who heralded in the 60s with protests and sit-ins that she and her friends were too young to join, but they still felt lucky to slide into the next decade on the coattails of their wild predecessors who were significantly changing the world.

Although they were all friends, Curtis took a special liking to Nicole. Curtis called it love, but Nicole called it—well, she was never sure what to call it. Curtis lived in a world of his own with a very active alter ego whose name he used as regularly as his real one. The three of them accepted Curtis' personality the same way they did each other's, and as different as Curtis and Nicole were from each other, everyone considered them boyfriend and girlfriend. The adult Nicole would realize one day that this—her first teenage romance—was rooted mostly in her attraction to his quirkiness. There was a darkness about Curtis that made Nicole uncomfortable but always drew her in at the same time. His manner towards her was often controlling and, at times, irrational, but because this was the first boy she ever dated, she didn't have another standard with which to compare his behavior. What she did know, however, was that she never felt compelled to spend hours expressing romantic feelings for Curtis to Diane, who was perpetually pining over John, another friend of the four.

Diane and Nicole were best friends and, like typical teenage girls, they shared secrets about their everyday lives and the adventures that might await them in the world outside their little town. And, of course, boys. Diane was hopelessly in love with John in a way that only hours of listening to Elton John and Joni Mitchell could cure. But Nicole had no such feelings for Curtis.

Garrett, on the other hand, was a different story. Garrett was gentle and kind and a musical genius. He played the piano in a way Nicole had never heard before, at least not like anyone her age. She, too, grew up taking piano lessons, and had earned high marks at several music competitions throughout her childhood, but she would never be able to play like Garrett. Garrett was drawn like a magnet to the piano wherever he found one. He was also one of those people who could simply hear a piece and play it. Nicole envied his ability, and like everyone else, was mesmerized by his gift. Though she didn't share his skill, Nicole had a deep connection to music the same way Garrett did.

Lately, Garrett's absence—from a room in someone's house or a classroom at school, on the weekend or during the week, anywhere, any time—was excruciating for Nicole. Nothing was the same when he wasn't around.

Whenever the foursome separated until they saw each other again the next day, the time in between was torture. Nicole had gotten fairly good at accepting the fact that she had to share Garrett with everyone else. After all, that's the way it had always been.

***

But today had been different. For whatever reason, the others couldn't join her and Garrett after school, so it was just the two of them. And now as the car turned onto the street of Nicole's house, she was about to say good-bye to Garrett again.

They pulled into the driveway. Garrett turned off the ignition and hopped out. *Say something*, Nicole told herself—anything to spend one more minute with him. Garrett ran around to the passenger side and opened the door.

"Can we still be friends?" he asked.

"What do you mean? We are friends."

He seemed tongue-tied, nervous, very unlike him, she thought. Maybe he was just cold. The vapor of his breath floated against the frigid air.

"We're moving."

Nicole rewound the tape in her head and played it back. She could have sworn he said, "We're moving."

"You're moving?"

Garrett nodded. "Yeah, back to Canada."

"Why?" *It's just a nightmare*, she thought. She would wake up in a moment.

"My dad's teaching thing is done."

"Oh." Nicole looked down at the doormat and pretended to kick the snow off her boots. "When?"

"Few weeks."

How could he sound so cheery when she was trying not to die right there in front of him? After all, Wishton was a nice little town. Most people seemed to like it here. What was not to like? From what little she knew of Garrett's family, they seemed happy here. Garrett had friends here. And *she* lived here.

"So, uhm, maybe we could write or something…" he mumbled.

Nicole didn't want to appear as though she weren't listening, but if she looked at him, he would see the tears in her eyes. She stared down at her boots.

"Yeah, sure," she said, fumbling for her house key. Before she could utter "good-bye," Garrett dashed back to his car.

Nicole went in the house, pulled off her boots, and ran straight upstairs to her bedroom. Slamming the door behind her, she threw herself on the bed and sobbed. It would be an hour later, when her mother called her down to dinner, before she realized she had never taken off her coat.

***

Garrett sat motionless with the motor running, the numbers and letters on the dashboard melting into a blur. He wiped the water from his eyes but the tiny particles of ice sticking to the wool threads of his glove were of little help. It would get better in a few minutes, he thought, as he steered away from Nicole's house. Meanwhile, trying to see tire tracks in the snow through tears was hell. He wiped his eyes again. All the glove did this time was make his cheeks sting.

It was the noble thing to do, not letting Nicole know how he felt about her. He thought of that song, 'The First Time Ever I Saw Your Face.' It reached into the listener's soul and now it was stuck in his head. He rummaged through a mound of cassettes until he found 'Fragile' by Yes, jammed it into the tape player and turned the volume up as high as it would go. The band's powerful, symphonic, classical style of rock had the perfect intensity to pound 'Roundabout' from the car speakers into Garrett's brain. By the time he got home, Roberta Flack's spiritually lilting voice would be gone from his head, and along with it, he hoped, any thoughts of Nicole.

Chapter Four

Where or When
Diana Krall, 2009

I tried to piece together the circumstances surrounding Liam's move back to Canada. The jokes about the dust that collects in the middle-aged brain were legitimate. How long had it been between the time he told me he was moving, and the time he actually left? Had some other boy caught my eye in the meantime? If so, had Liam watched from the wings? Or worse, had Liam started dating some other girl at school? To hell with it. I didn't like thinking either of us may have had eyes for anyone but each other. The only significant element was that the time I spent with Liam before he moved away had been remarkably short. It was the stuff old Hollywood movies and classic love songs and Shakespeare were made of— that brief, intensely magical moment when you meet another person and the experience slips through your hand as quickly as you're aware of it. Yet even now, decades later, I could still remember how I felt every moment I was with him, and the overwhelming sadness that came over me whenever we parted. I could, of course, simply fast forward to create a world where our separation never took place, sparing my brain the frustration of trying to remember, and my heart a ton of emotional anguish in the process. But our separation was the foundation for the story. It was what made the story worth writing. And now, it was the source of the electric current that shot through my veins whenever I saw a message from Liam.

LIAM: Hey there, pretty lady.

MIRANDA: Hi!

LIAM: What are you up to?

MIRANDA: Not much, what about you?

LIAM: About to go into another meeting.
Was thinking about you.

MIRANDA: I'm having trouble remembering something.
Maybe you can help me.

LIAM: Shoot.

MIRANDA: Was it Christmas Eve or Christmas Day
that you showed up at my
house to take me out?

LIAM: It was Christmas Day.

We walked around downtown
and then went to a movie.

MIRANDA: I remember walking around
but I don't remember going to a movie!

LIAM: The movie was terrible.
You were magical.

MIRANDA: You're sweet.

LIAM: I was smitten.

MIRANDA: My most vivid memory of that day is
the snowflakes floating in front of your eyes
and those adorable frameless
glasses you wore.
And the bluest eyes I'd ever seen.

LIAM: They're still blue, by the way.

MIRANDA: I assumed so.

LIAM: We kissed and I floated
on air the whole way home.

MIRANDA: Stop.

LIAM: It's true.

MIRANDA: I have a confession to make.

LIAM: Which is?

MIRANDA: I was in love with you.

LIAM: Awww.

MIRANDA: Oh, c'mon! You mean you didn't know?

LIAM: I secretly hoped.

MIRANDA: LOL.

LIAM: I was in love with you, too.

MIRANDA: Wonder why you—we—didn't
tell each other?

LIAM: You were my best friend's girl.

MIRANDA: You mean, you did the noble thing?

LIAM: Absolutely. I suffered in silence.

MIRANDA: That sounds like how I remember you.
Always the gentleman… and the goofball.

LIAM: Nothing's changed on either account.

MIRANDA: LOL—I can tell.
I'm just kinda sad that I spent all that

time with Louis when I should have been
with you. What an idiot I was.

LIAM: Don't be so hard on yourself. We were kids.

MIRANDA: You were supposed to say,
Miranda, you were never an idiot.

LIAM: Okay. Don't be so hard on yourself.
We were kids.

MIRANDA: Wise ass!

LIAM: Didn't you just say I hadn't changed?

MIRANDA: Indeed, I did… sigh.

LIAM: Gotta go, love.

MIRANDA: Bye. Wait—one more thing!

LIAM: Yes?

MIRANDA: Did you tell me the other day
you had three brothers?

LIAM: Yep.

MIRANDA: I didn't remember that. My husband
has three brothers, too. I just think that's a
funny coincidence, ya know?

LIAM: That is funny!

MIRANDA: Where are you in the birth order?

LIAM: I'm the youngest. It's Jim, then Brian,
then Walker, then me.

I froze when I saw the names. Two of Neil's brothers were also named James and Brian. I didn't share that part with Liam. He would probably think it was just another funny coincidence. But to me, it rattled even louder my belief in a parallel existence where Liam's soul was connected to mine. Right in the middle of that thought, I felt the tug. It was that reality tug that showed up every time I wanted to visit the place where I preferred to hang out—Dreamland. For the most part, there was nothing at all wrong with Dreamland. Everybody spent time there now and then—and if they didn't, they should. Dreamland was at the core of all creativity, all art. It was the place from which not only art, but great inventions were conjured, where all ideas began. Occasionally, my visits to Dreamland were followed by an obligatory visit to the mirror. I put down the iPhone and stood at the vanity in the bathroom.

"The man I believe is my soul mate and the man I married are both one of four brothers and their brothers have the same names?" I asked the image in the glass.

The word *MIRACULOUS* appeared in cursive, purplish, velvety letters across the mirror. Then with some imaginary eraser, the letters were wiped away and re-placed by the words *OR MEANT TO BE*, followed by a question mark.

Meant to be? Meaning I should accept that the stars over my head on the day I was born got mixed up? Like the original blueprint of my life came with intentional sets of circumstances unintentionally assigned to the wrong people? More simply, or more profoundly, that God made some kind of mistake? I didn't believe God made mistakes any more than I believed in coincidences.

"Where's the camera that's filming this? 'Cuz it's too unbelievable to be true," I sighed.

The imaginary eraser rubbed the words away again, re-placed, this time, by *RELAX. ENJOY THE RIDE.*

I was starting to like whoever was drawing those pur-plish, velvety letters.

Chapter Five

Truly
Lionel Richie, 1982

*D*ear Garrett,

How do you like being back in Canada? It's really weird not seeing you in study hall. John keeps telling the same old stupid jokes at lunch and I wish he would stop. It's so boring with you gone. It's really fun being editor of the Eagle and if Mr. G lets me, I'd love to do it again next year. I'm thinking about majoring in journalism instead of drama. Plus, I really like to write. Mother keeps telling me I'm good at it and that I used to write stories when I was six years old. Anyway, for now I can still be in the spring musical so I can do both. I know I'll probably only get chorus, as usual, and either Jenny Brent or Linda Rhineman will get the female lead, of course, but that's okay.

I really had fun when we went out on Christmas Day. It was the best Christmas I ever had! I didn't tell anyone about it, not even Diane. I didn't want her to tell John because then John would tell Curtis. If you told Curtis, he never said anything about it. Anyway, I had a really good time and I didn't want it to end. Too bad the movie was so bad! When are you coming back to visit? Sometimes my Mom and Dad and my Uncle Dave and Aunt Linda like to go to Toronto just for the weekend. I think they're going during spring break. I usually stay with my Aunt Ava when they go up there but maybe they could take me with them this time so I can come visit you!

Miss you lots! Write back soon,
Love,
Nicole

***

D*ear Nicole,*

It's great being back! You should definitely come up with your folks for a visit. You would love it here! There's so much to see and do in Toronto. Did you know my family has a side business with the Toronto Chamber of Commerce giving sight-seeing tours, and I'm the youngest docent in the history of the city to ever earn the title of tour guide? Just kidding!! But we can still have a blast! I had a great time Christmas Day, too. I didn't tell Curtis. I like the way my face looks and he might have rearranged it.

Let me know as soon as you know for sure about Spring break.
Miss you too,
Love,
Garrett
PS: Don't be too hard on John. Not everyone can be as witty as me!

***

T oronto was truly an amazing city. As the cab driver pulled over to the curb outside the entrance to High Park, Nicole could barely contain her excitement.

"Don't forget," her father said. "Back at the hotel by five-thirty."

"Okay," said Nicole as she peered through the throngs of pedestrians. Suddenly she saw Garrett, wearing a bright blue jacket and plaid cap just like he told her. "There he is!"

"You be careful," her mom warned as Nicole hopped out. Garrett made his way towards her with a beaming smile. Nicole threw her arms around him. He wanted the feeling of her nose tucked in the crook of his neck to last an eternity. A boisterous shout from inside the cab interrupted the tight squeeze he had on Nicole's tiny frame.

"How are you, Mr. McKinnon?" Nicole's mom said through the car window.

"Hey, Ms. Martin! I'm grand! Hey, Mr. Martin!"

Nicole's dad poked his head out from around the other side of his wife's shoulder and returned a cheerful,

"Good to see you!"

"Hey, Ms. Martin, you still teaching?" Garrett asked.

"What are you talking about? Of course I'm still teaching. You thought I'd retired already?"

"Well, I thought maybe since I left WHS it was too depressing for you to set foot inside of it anymore," grinned Garrett.

May Martin threw her head back and laughed. She was the teacher that parents wanted their kids and their kids' siblings to get once they got to Wishton High. Her passionate affair with education was in its twenty-fifth year and had brought all kinds of students through the doors of her English class over the years, some thirsting to learn, some not, but each and every one of them loving her for her fierce fairness and her unforgettable round-faced smile and for the depth with which they knew she genuinely cared about them as human beings. And she loved each of them equally in return, from the shyest to the loudest, from the most remedial to the most genius. But the Garrett McKinnons of the world were the kind of student whose sense of humor May Martin and her colleagues looked forward to every day, despite the stress and administrative politics that came with their occupation. The added bonus, of course, was that Garrett's type was also incredibly smart, making him a challenge to teach, and May always harbored a twinge of jealousy that her best friend Charlotte Sherman was the one who got the sharp-witted kid from Canada for English Comp and Lit 03.

"You two stay out of trouble," warned May, content that the teenagers would understand her comment's various meanings.

"Aye-aye, captain," Garrett replied, raising his hand to his forehead in a military salute. The cab pulled away from the curb and Garrett grabbed Nicole's hand. "C'mon!"

The brisk April air nipped at Nicole's cheeks and she grew nearly out of breath keeping up with Garrett's pace. As the local resident teenager and his foreign-born companion maneuvered their way through the immense crowd the sunny day had drawn to High Park, they turned a bend and Nicole let out a gasp. Before her was a stunning display of white cherry blossom trees for as far as she could see. Garrett had been right about playing tour guide. If he wasn't completely in love with this city, he was certainly in love with this particular place.

"Ever seen a bison up close?" he asked.

"I've never seen a bison at all," Nicole giggled.

"Oh, then you're in for a treat. Wait till you see them, they're enormous." They approached the zoo section of the park. Nicole loved zoos and she was as excited as a five year old.

"I wanna see the lions!" she said.

"Won't find any of those here, sorry. Not that kind of zoo."

"Oh."

"You hungry?"

"A little."

"You wanna eat first?"

"No, it's okay. We can eat later."

"Ok. So, first, bison. Then, lunch?"

"Bison. Lunch," Nicole echoed.

"No, not a bison lunch!" he quipped. "They won't let you eat them! You're only allowed to look at them."

Nicole giggled again and shook her head at his silliness. It was at that moment she realized just how much she'd missed him. He squeezed her hand a little tighter as they strolled through the park. Even the disapproving glances they received from parents at the petting zoo didn't stop them from wedging past the pint-sized guests for a turn to feed the baby animals. Only once did they stop to rest, but not before finding the perfect spot beneath the perfect tree, that in the stillness of its beauty, begged to be the one the two would choose. They enjoyed a meal of ham and cheese sandwiches and made up stories about passers-by. Had Nicole ever been this happy?

"How soon do you have to get back?" Garrett asked.

Nicole rolled her eyes. "I told you three times, already! Five-thirty."

"Oh, right. I was just hoping if I kept asking, the answer might change."

"To what?" she asked.

"To 'never.'"

"Never?"

"Yeah. Stay here."

"I can't. I have something called school, ya know."

"They have schools here. I can prove it." Nicole rolled her eyes at him again. "Tell your folks you wanna move to Canada."

"Tell your folks you wanna move back to Wishton."

"But I don't," Garrett replied.

Nicole's jaw dropped open. She socked him on the arm.

"You're only going to be there one more year anyway," Garrett said. "Then you'll be graduating. Where do you want to go after?"

"Mmmm… I really want to go to Carnegie Mellon."

"Oh, ya. For theatre, right?"

"Yeah."

The two teenagers were unaware of how many minutes passed while they sat under their tree. Nicole's back was propped against it, her slender, blue-jeaned legs stretched out in front of her on the fragrant grass, Garrett across from her. When he suddenly reclined on his back, laying his head in her lap, she was certain every living thing in the park could hear her heart beating.

She looked at his face in a different way this time from how she'd ever looked at him before. The awkwardness she'd always felt in the past whenever they were alone together was gone. The excitement she'd always felt was still there, but mysteriously overpowered by something else, something deeper. It was as though she drank in his spirit. She felt it pour down into her core and she felt her spirit pour into his. It was a feeling that embraced the good in all things, and didn't belong only to the present moment, but had its origin from another time. It was not a time from their past, nor a time in their future; it was timeless.

Nicole didn't need to look up at the sky to know Garrett's eyes were following the flight pattern of two baby starlings, and next, a whimsical, down-filled pillow-shaped cloud formation. He subconsciously took her hand and tucked it inside both of his, and rested it tenderly against his chest. She could feel his heart beating, and it brought hers to a normal, tranquil pace. Years later, Garrett would sit on this same hill in this same park, and meditate beneath this same tree. And the memory of this day would return to his consciousness with even greater joy than his young soul was able to appreciate right now.

Chapter Six

So Far Away
Carole King, 1971

Nicole didn't say a word the entire car ride back to Wishton. Her parents repeatedly asked what was wrong, and she repeatedly answered "nothing," but May suspected Nicole's mood had everything to do with leaving Garrett. It would be that way for the next few years. A reunion, followed by a separation, followed by a reunion, and then another separation, punctuated by her own high school graduation. Throughout college, the couple boys with whom there was a possibility of a relationship never seemed to get past the 'friendship' phase with Nicole. Through no fault of their own, they simply weren't Garrett. Friends told her she was crazy to hold out for a commitment with a long distance boyfriend, but she and Garrett continued to see each other as often as vacation from their respective colleges would allow. When they did, their visits were so magical, so fulfilling, that Garrett was always *with her* long after he wasn't *with her*. How could anyone expect her to let that go, especially after that summer they spent a week together taking a train through the Canadian Rockies? It was on that trip that Nicole lost her virginity.

***

"I want to make love to you," Garrett whispered in her ear.

The confession perched Nicole on a precipice of her womanhood from which she knew there'd be no return, sending her mind spinning and heart reeling, unsure whether she was really ready for the so-this-is-what-all-the-love-songs-are-about moment. They were alone in a clearing of larch trees they'd found far away from one of the walking trails. Arms and legs wrapped around each other inside one sleeping bag, they could feel the ground beneath them growing cooler since nightfall, despite the wool plaid horse blanket they'd placed between the turf and their cocoon. Their awareness of the extremely hard and increasingly uncomfortable spot they'd chosen was second to the extremely hard and increasingly uncomfortable erection inside Garrett's jeans.

"I want to make love to you, too," Nicole said.

Garrett traced Nicole's face with his fingers as he spoke, as though he were seeing its features for the first time.

"You're beautiful, you know that?" he said.

She smiled.

"Are you sure you want to do it?" he asked her.

"Yeah. Don't you?"

"Of course I do. I've been wanting to for a long time."

"Me, too. I wanted… well, I didn't want to do it with anyone else but you," she blushed.

A look of worry wove across his brow.

"What's wrong?" Nicole asked.

"Nothing. I just…"

"Is that bad? That I saved myself for you? I thought you'd be happy."

"No—I am."

"Then why do you look so serious all of a sudden?"

"It's… that makes me feel really special," although, responsible, was closer to what he was feeling.

"I love you. I don't remember a time when I didn't love you. Like it's timeless or something. Like you came to me in a dream and I'm still in it."

"Well, this should be really special and the only romantic thing I have to offer is all those stars above us," Garrett whispered.

"Good job. They're beautiful."

"Let's pretend they're just for us."

"Okay."

"Shh!" Garrett whispered.

"What?"

"I think I heard something," Garrett said.

Nicole froze, afraid to move her head to look around, instead, taking all cues from Garrett's face.

"Do you think someone's coming?" she whispered.

"I don't know. Nothing human, anyway."

Nicole gasped.

"There are bears out here, ya know," Garrett informed her.

"What?!" Nicole replied, eyes wide.

"Shh, shh, shh!" Garrett didn't move a muscle. Then, "No, I'm kidding."

"You think scaring me like that is romantic?"

"Sorry."

"Why do you have to do that?" asked Nicole.

"I don't have to. I just like to."

"Why, though?"

"Because you're just so adorable when I tease you."

"What a mood kill."

"Wait—what?"

"You killed the mood."

"I did?" Garrett replied, unsure if she was joking. "You mean you don't want to do it anymore?"

"Well, I did, but I'm kinda worried about bears now," Nicole pouted, lowering her eyelids coyly.

Garrett picked up on the tease. "No, you're not!"

"Wait, did you bring it?"

"What?"

"Did you bring a condom?"

"Oh no!"

"You're kidding, right?"

"Yes," Garrett whispered in her ear.

He pressed his lips against hers as he slipped his hand under her sweatshirt. His hand felt cool against her warm, bare skin, and her torso beckoned with delightful anticipation his hand's upward journey to where her soft breasts were waiting. Soon she knew his hands would be everywhere, like every time before. But this time, the ending would be different. She was nervous, excited, a little scared. Some of her girlfriends said it hurt the first time.

But there was only one thing she knew for sure: she had never, ever trusted another human being so completely.

"I love you, Nicky."

***

Nicole had a professor who said, "if you don't want the answer, then don't ask the question," so she made a point not to ask Garrett too much about his dating practices. She didn't want to accept the fact that while they were apart, he might not be spending all his nights alone. He was, after all, a 'guy.' So she told herself if it happened, it was okay, because that's what guys do, right? She also told herself she should stop telling herself that, because no matter how much she did, it didn't make her feel any better. He'd admitted to going out with a couple girls now and then, but said he was committed to Nicole. That's all that mattered to her, and she'd left it at that.

One month before college graduation, the producers of a network daytime drama in New York came to Carnegie Mellon. Most of the students in the acting program scoffed at the opportunity, saying television was beneath them, and soap operas were beneath television. But ever since she was five years old, delivering touching performances to her mirror as various Disney princesses, all Nicole ever wanted to do when she grew up was be on a TV soap opera and live in a big house in Hollywood. She'd never allowed peer pressure to dictate her choices (as the daughter of a school teacher, the pressure was *not* to give in to peer pressure), but the looks from her fellow theatre students were anything but supportive when they

40

saw Nicole's name (and only three others) on the sign-up sheet on the department's bulletin board. She asked the vocal instructor (as in the use of the voice as the instrument for verbal communication—not as in singing) Ms. Hamilton, what she should do. Ms. Hamilton was a brilliant woman who was part love child from the Hippie era, part academic genius, and one of those people with whom you could share anything.

"I think you should do what your heart tells you to do," Hamilton advised in the slow, melodic, gossamer tones that were her natural method of speaking. Nicole was certain that in the privacy of her own home, Hamilton pulled off the human disguise she wore for the rest of the world, revealing a real live angel underneath.

On the day of the audition, Nicole slipped on her high-heeled pumps, straightened her spine, and delivered what she felt was the best audition of her life. The role was for a young ingénue struggling to balance love and career—not too much of a stretch.

Two weeks later, she got a phone call from the production company.

"Is this Nicole?"

"Yes."

"This is Bailey Edwards from 'Don't Look Back.'"

"Oh my goodness, yes, hi!"

"Our producers want to offer you the role of Lisa if you're still interested."

"Oh my God!"

"How soon can you move to New York?"

Her first call was to her parents, and the second was to Garrett. Nicole would never know how much her news broke his heart. He was her biggest fan, her sweetheart and best friend, and he was thrilled for her. But Garrett had no interest in moving to New York, and the situation would perpetuate the long distance relationship they thought was behind them.

Chapter Seven

Sorry Seems to Be the Hardest Word
Elton John, 1976

The rain was torrential and Nicole felt increasingly nauseous as the bus seemed to take forever to get to the university. She kicked herself for not taking a cab instead, but she had taken this particular shuttle from the airport a dozen times and saw no reason not to do it this time. The whole thing was a bad idea from the start, promising Garrett she would be there. But how could she not? It was the biggest opportunity of his young career. As a distinguished graduate of their music program, he'd been invited as the guest pianist for the University of Toronto's opening of their new concert hall, and would be accompanied by a full orchestra. The time he'd spent practicing until his fingers nearly bled had become an integral part of their time together. His music was the third person in their love affair, the only thief Nicole would allow to steal him from her bed. She loved watching him practice and loved hearing him play and it had all led to this night. But her rehearsal at the studio ran late and she missed her flight out of LaGuardia. It was over an hour before she could get the next one to Toronto.

The bus came to a halt and Nicole jumped out into the rain. She was still a block from the music building. There was very little activity about. No doubt the nasty weather had kept folks inside. She broke into a trot against the slippery pavement, but what was the point? The concert started at 7:00 p.m. It was almost nine o'clock now. How would she ever make it up to him? They had planned to go out and celebrate after the performance, so maybe he'd still be there. She hadn't bothered to call him to tell him she missed the flight because he would have already left home. Another fly in the ointment.

Nicole ran up to the glass doors of the concert hall and tugged on the handles. Locked. *Of course*, she thought. But the lights in the lobby were still on. She spotted an usher closing up a concession stand. She banged on the door. The woman sauntered over.

"We're locked up, ma'am."

"Is there anyone still in there?" Nicole shouted through the glass.

"Someone's in there playing the piano." The woman yawned.

"Can you please let me in?"

"I told you, these doors are locked."

"Can't you unlock them? Please?" Nicole pleaded. The usher rolled her eyes.

"Go around there to your left and I'll let you in the side door," she pointed.

Nicole ran to the side of the building to a steel door that said 'Artist's Entrance.' Seconds later the usher opened it and Nicole dashed inside. There was the faint sound of a piano coming from the auditorium. "That's him! My boyfriend. How do I get in there?"

"Balcony. Straight ahead. Stairs are on your left."

Nicole raced down a short hallway and up the stairs. Why were there so many of them? As she climbed as fast as she could, drops of water from the tip of her umbrella left a straight line of tiny crystals on the burgundy colored carpeted steps. She could hear Garrett's playing more audibly now. She yanked open the first balcony door she came to. The auditorium was dark. There he was, at the piano, alone on the massive stage. Out of breath, she collapsed in a seat on the first row of the balcony.

"Garrett!" she called down to him.

He stopped playing for a second but didn't look up. She wished she were anyone but herself right now. This was not going to be an easy conversation.

"You're not even going to look at me?" she asked.

Finally, he shot her a glance, but then went back to playing the piano.

"Oh, hi, Nicole," he said, overwhelmingly pleasant. So that's how he was going to play this, she thought. Typical. Now she'd have to cut through his exacerbating politeness in addition to the sound of the piano.

"Garrett! Can you please stop?" she shouted.

He stopped playing and stared up at her. He didn't say a word, and what seemed like an eternity passed before she said anything either.

"I missed my flight. I took the very next one I could get and maybe I should have tried to call you but…"

The look on his face was not anger, not hurt, but something else. She wasn't sure what his expression meant, but it made her feel pathetic. "I'm sorry."

He started to play again.

"My God! Stop playing the piano!" Nicole yelled.

Garrett put his hands in his lap and looked up at her, saying nothing for a moment. Finally, he spoke. "Why are you here? The concert's over."

She preferred to ignore the remark. But she knew she may as well face the music. "Okay, I know you hate me right now and maybe you don't even want to see me, but can you at least—can we just—go home?"

"You mean 'home,' as in, my apartment? Cuz that's my home. I live here. You live in New York. With all your obligations."

Nicole's abdomen received the dagger. But she didn't want to have this conversation right now, and certainly not here. At that moment the usher's voice drifted in from the left wing of the stage.

"Sir, I have to lock up the building in a minute."

Garrett closed the piano. Nicole took a deep breath and walked out of the balcony.

***

The loft apartment in the newly renovated part of Liberty Village was one of Nicole's favorite places. At one side was Garrett's piano, surrounded by stacks of music books, sheet music, hand-written notes and two metronomes—a basic store-bought one that Garrett actually used, and the one his grandmother had given him when he was a little boy. It was a cherished heirloom that he placed in a spot where he would always see it. Scattered about were some of Garrett's favorite books: *Carl Sagan's Cosmic Connection, Lord of the Rings, Atlas Shrugged, Beethoven: The Last Decade*. There was an old TV from college that he refused to replace, a stereo with an impressive set of speakers, and a small coffee table strewn with cassette tapes. Amid these items were a couple cups of unfinished coffee.

On the other side of the room was a queen sized sofa bed whose sheets Nicole was nestled in at the moment. Snuggled against the crook of her back was Gin, the Russian Blue that she had given to Garrett when she moved to New York a year ago. Her landlord didn't allow pets, and it broke her heart to separate from the cat, but she knew he'd get all the love he needed in Garrett's care. The energy that flowed within this space was a mixture of Garrett's creative side and his love of science. Nicole felt completely at home inside its walls, not just because she was 'the girlfriend who had a key,' but perhaps because she, too, was born with the artist vs. analyst gene, a dichotomy that would plague her for her entire life.

Needless to say the tension was thick when they got back to the loft the night before. Garrett hated it whenever she tried to make excuses, so she hadn't. They didn't make love, which they always did the instant they saw each other after being apart, and she hadn't expected them to under the circumstances. He'd opened up a little about the concert, but Garrett was overly critical when it came to his own talent, so Nicole knew that no matter what he said, his performance was better than his assessment.

She climbed out of bed and pulled on the faded pink terry cloth robe she kept at his place. Garrett was already in the kitchenette making a pot of coffee. As usual first thing in the morning, the only thing he was wearing were his favorite pair of sweatpants. They were old and baggy and loosely covered the bottom half of his slender frame. It was so sexy the way those particular pants hung below the top of his pelvis, allowing a frontal view of that marked indentation on the male anatomy just above… she needed to focus. They had to have a serious talk and they needed to get straight to the point. No preamble. No editorializing. It was a recurring topic but this time Nicole wanted a solution. She wanted to change things.

"This long distance thing isn't working."

Garrett handed her a cup of coffee. "For who?"

"What do you mean 'for who?' For us. Us living apart. It's not working."

"It's not that far. About nine hours by car, a little over one, by plane."

"Yes, I know, but—"

"Minuscule, compared to, let's say, from here to Dubai."

"Okay, if you just want to crack jokes—"

"Wasn't the intention."

"The point is, I don't want what happened last night to ever happen again."

"But it did. Let's move on," Garrett said.

"You want to move on, Garrett? You want to just pretend you're not hurt that I missed the biggest performance of your life and I'll pretend I don't know how hurt you are? And how I feel like a piece of shit because it's my fault?"

"Shit happens."

"Yes, I know. But I don't want to move on. I want to eliminate the risk of what happened last night from ever happening again. And I can't control my taping schedule. So, I guess what I'm asking is…" a chilly glance from Garrett slowing her down "… no more flights back and forth?"

Gin's rhythmic purring was the only sound in the loft as the couple sipped on their coffees. Nicole didn't know what Garrett was going to say, but past conversations on the subject indicated he didn't like this long distance relationship any more than she did.

"You want me to move to New York," he said flatly.

"Do you have a better solution?" she replied.

"Why don't you move to Toronto?" he asked.

That was a tough one. Nicole had only been on the soap for five months, a rare win for an acting student fresh out of college. Leaving New York right now would be career suicide.

"It's not that I'd never consider it. I told you before, I would. But the timing sucks right now. I'm taping at least four days a week and it looks like they're developing my character and that usually means I'll be in the story line for a while. And that's a good thing."

"I've got a job, too, ya know."

He was talking about his position at de Havilland, the major aircraft manufacturer where he worked as a products assistant. He liked it there and made a respectable wage that more than covered his rent and allowed him enough flexibility to pursue his music. What Nicole said next would sound selfish no matter how she worded it, so she just blurted it out.

"I can't leave New York right now. Please move to New York so we can be together?"

She looked at him hoping that, in her eyes, he'd see her pleading for him to trust her. She watched the wheels turning behind his blue pools, searching for a guarantee, grappling with an answer, teetering on the edge of a decision he might regret, either way. It was his least favorite position to be in. But he knew by the look on her face that she was serious this time. And he also knew, deep down inside, how much she loved him. For a second it seemed as if he were about to utter something, but it was only a silent breath of air floating between his parted lips. *Please don't change the subject*, Nicole prayed.

Garrett strolled past her to the piano, sat down and started to play. She knew better than to intersect him and his music when he was drawn to it, so she went back to the sofa bed and curled up in the middle of it. As Gin continuously readjusted to find the warmest place on Nicole's frame, Nicole wished she could read Garrett's mind. But that was never going to happen. So she closed her eyes and let herself be caressed by the melody that flowed from his fingertips, content that all that mattered at the moment was that he hadn't said, "No."

Chapter Eight

Nicole reached the second story of the Upper West Side brownstone and made her way down the hallway of the little abode she and Garrett had chosen together. Like most apartments in New York, theirs was tiny but functional: too small to have more than two friends over at a time, but big enough that they could avoid bumping into each other if both of them were home. There was only one problem. There was no room for a piano. Garrett had told her it was okay, but she hadn't believed it for a minute. She promised him that if her acting career took off the way she hoped, they'd soon be able to afford a place with all the space they ever wanted. For the time being, the modest apartment served its purpose. It wasn't too far by subway to the studio, and only a few minutes from NYU, where Garrett found a job as a teaching assistant in the planetary studies department. It was a place where he had access to all the resources he could get his hands on to feed his fascination with the vastness of the universe, along with an endless stream of world class lecturers coming through to speak on the topic.

Balancing a full bag of groceries, Nicole stumbled through the door and found Garrett sitting on the floor surrounded by a half dozen moving boxes they still had to unpack. She lowered her lips to his for a quick kiss hello and carried their dinner into the kitchen.

"This is really good," he said.

"What's that?" she asked, her head inside the fridge.

"The play you wrote."

Nicole's stomach did a flip. He was talking about *Dear Teresa, I Love You*, inspired by the time Curtis stalked her after she went away to college. Garrett's comment conjured the first time she got a glimpse of Curtis' face in the rear view mirror of the car the night she and a couple friends drove into downtown. She'd been sure she was seeing things. Wasn't Curtis back home in Wishton? Her parents had even mentioned seeing him around town. After Garrett moved away and the rest of their gang graduated high school, any ties Nicole had with Curtis were severed. But soon after the night she thought she spotted him sitting in the parked car behind them, the letters started to arrive. Though Nicole was never sure how Curtis had gotten her address.

The letters were multiple pages in length, hand-written, and always started out the same way: declaring how much Curtis loved her. Each one was more passionate than the last, and read like a rambling stream of consciousness about how he owned Nicole, mind, body and soul, and how she was his most precious possession.

They also implied a sexual relationship between Curtis and Nicole, when in reality their courtship was never consummated. After a while, their daily arrival in the mail became a routine joke among Nicole's roommates.

And then, there was that one letter. The one that, when Nicole read it, she instantly knew that Curtis' state of mind was anything but funny. The one that said, *We'll be together, even in death.* If Curtis was fixated on a union between them, alive or dead, and he was there in Pittsburgh, could she be in danger? The thought made her sick. She became afraid to go to class and afraid to stay home. When someone left a single white rose on the doormat outside the apartment, Nicole was certain Curtis had been there. The smart thing to do was call the police, she thought, so she did. They told her that because the harassing behavior occurred via the U.S. Mail, it would be a matter for the FBI. Not long after that, the Feds paid Curtis a visit back in Wishton, and Nicole never heard from him again.

Nicole didn't know there was such a thing as 'psychological rape' until she'd been a victim of it, and channeled her feelings onto paper by writing a play. She'd even staged a reading of it with some of her actor friends, but it went no further. And it was a memory that, no matter how eloquently portrayed, was one she wanted to bury forever. Now Garrett had found the script and was applauding her work. She knew she should be appreciative, but all she felt was resentment.

"Thanks," she said.

"I never knew you wrote a play," replied Garrett.

"Yep."

"It's gripping."

"I know, you said that already."

"No, I said it's 'good.'"

"Okay, it's good. You find it good. You think it's gripping. I don't want to talk about it."

"Okay," said Garrett, unsure of his offense. He closed the manuscript and tossed it back on top of the box where it came from.

"That's all you have to say?" Nicole snapped.

"I thought you didn't want to talk about it."

"I don't!" she fired. "Not the play!"

Now, he was confused. "Then, what?"

"Did you know?"

"Know what?"

"Did you know he did that to me?"

"That he stalked you?"

"Yes! That he followed me to Pittsburgh, that he scared the shit out of me, that he threatened to kill me!"

"All I knew was…"

"What?"

"… what he told me."

"Which was?"

"Which was, that he might go visit you. That's all he ever said."

"And you let him?"

"What was I supposed to do? I wasn't his babysitter. I didn't even live in Wishton anymore."

"You should have protected me!" Nicole shouted.

"Bullshit!" The words stung her. He recognized that look on her face when she didn't want to hear the truth about something. The look that revealed the tug of war between her vulnerability and her strength, and always made him love her more. His next words were slow, tender.

"Since the day I met you, I've wanted to protect you. From everything. What was I supposed to say to him? 'Don't you dare go see her, you bastard—oh, sorry, I mean, *best friend*—cuz I'm in love with her and I'll bash your fuckin' skull in if you go anywhere near her?'"

"Telling him that would've sounded pretty wonderful, actually," Nicole said.

"Maybe in a movie."

"Well, congratulations, he could have killed me."

"Oh, c'mon, don't be so dramatic."

"You're denying it?"

"What—that he could've killed you?"

"Yes."

"Okay, he could have killed you. Is that what you want me to say?"

"He *could* have!"

"Yes, I know he could have killed you, Nicky! He nearly killed himself, which is why he's in the loony bin now."

Silence filled the walls of their tiny space. Nicole sank down on the floor like a wounded puppy, holding her face in her hands. Garrett scooted next to her and wrapped his arms around her.

"I'm sorry he did that to you. I never knew how sick he was. And it was kind of hard to protect you when you were so far away. I'd have given anything to have you with me, but I knew your heart was set on Carnegie. Maybe I couldn't protect you, but I promised I'd wait for you… Why are you crying?"

Nicole shrugged her shoulders as if to say, "I don't know."

"Nicky, if it makes you cry then why are we even talking about it?"

"I didn't bring it up, you did," she sniffled.

"All I said was that I thought the play you wrote was really good." Garrett held her tighter. "And besides, if you wanted me to protect you, where's the scene where I come dashing in on a white horse, wearing shining armor? And I slay Curtis? And the crowd cheers? And then I go to remove my helmet, and it gets stuck, and I can't get it off my head?"

"Great. Now my psychological drama is a comedy," Nicole said through her tears.

"No, that's just the comic relief."

"The comic relief?"

"Yeah."

"Wait, you can't have live horses on stage."

"Yeah, you can."

"I mean, yeah, you can, but, if I did—I mean—if I did this, I don't see it having a budget to have live horses on stage. Besides, that's way over the top."

"Okay, then, maybe in the movie version."

"You think it's good enough to be made into a movie?"

"No."

Nicole socked him hard on the arm.

"Ow!" Garrett grimaced.

"I'm just comic-reliefing…"

"Anyway, so I come riding in on a white horse—"

"What color is Curtis' horse?"

"I don't know. His can't be white. He's the villain. I'm the hero. I'm the one that gets the white one, ya?"

"Guess he gets a black one."

"I don't know—black, chestnut, Palamino—you have to be creative, Nicky. Don't go for the obvious choice."

"Okay. But you're on a white one. That's not obvious?"

"Well, okay, maybe just a little. Anyway, so there's a big sword fight and I slay Curtis but it's all for nothing because I can't get any credit 'cause no one knows it's me underneath the helmet."

"Cuz you can't get it off."

"Yeessss." A ridiculous ear to ear grin plastered itself proudly across Garrett's face.

"Why is that a good thing?" asked Nicole.

"It's not. It's just funny."

Nicole gazed lovingly at Garrett and realized, like so many times before, because of something he'd said, she was no longer crying.

"Why are you looking at me like that?" he asked her.

She took his face in her hands and kissed him gently on the lips.

"I would know it's you," she said. "That's all that matters."

Chapter Nine

Miss You
The Rolling Stones, 1978

With my head poised over it, I clung to the toilet seat with both hands. I hadn't vomited this violently since I was pregnant with Cassandra. At least there was not the slightest chance of that being the case. No man had touched me in over two years. Liam talked about wanting to touch me. I shook off the memory of one conversation in particular before it had the chance to return in detail. Becoming aroused while you're vomiting was not a feeling I wanted to experience. I knew what was making me sick was stress from a place I prayed to avoid, from feelings I never thought would take hold of me, from emotions I vowed I'd control. Even Liam told me to stop looking for logic where matters of the heart were concerned. Easy for him to say. But if I'd listened to him, would I be in a heap on the bathroom floor right now like a college kid with a hangover? Was I wrong to try to make sense of what our relationship was becoming? The immediate circumstances were plain and simple but in the movie I'd pictured for my life, they were ridiculous.

"This is insanity," I found myself whispering out loud. "This is why there are so many songs and books and poems written about this. True love, it's crazy. I'm crazy…" *Oh, gee, what if I really am crazy?*

I ran a washcloth under cold water and wiped my face. The purplish, velvety letters in the mirror were not so kind this time.

GET A FUCKING GRIP.

But thirty hours had passed since I'd heard from Liam and I was falling apart. The last time we spoke, I was the one who'd initiated it. When we did finally connect, the conversation was brief. When he said, "Gotta go," all I could think was, *Please, don't.* Or, had it been more like, *Stay and pay attention to me, dammit. How dare you have a life?*

"You're not afraid of flying," Liam had said to me recently. "You're afraid of not being in control."

Maybe he was right. Maybe it was just that I wanted to be in control. And when the whole mind-spinning scenario with him began, I was fairly sure I had been. It felt deliriously decadent, at first. But now, I felt like Alice falling down the Rabbit Hole. Alice falling down the Rabbit Hole felt uncertain, almost treacherous, and there was nothing that felt good about that. In any event, I'd be damned if I were going to take full responsibility for it.

It was only fair that Liam share fifty percent of the blame. After all, he was the one who had said the word *love* first, and for him, *love* wasn't just a word. I knew that like I knew my own face in the mirror. He'd said the word *want* first, too, and oh, the luscious phrases he'd used to make that clear. Didn't he realize he'd reached inside my gut with a hold that wouldn't let go? If only he knew I'd never felt this good. *You're perfect*, was the phrase he'd used only a week ago. If only he could see me now—an absolute hot mess because I'd fallen in love with him. Again. Liam Kincaid was back in my life with more than a snowfall on a Christmas Day when we were babies, and I was his answer to something, though I wasn't exactly sure what it was. Nor did I care, really. I was too busy loving that I was *it*.

But I was the one who'd said the word *need* first. And now, like a baby bearing the pain of its first tooth, I didn't like it. It was an ugly process that makes the baby cry. I'd helplessly watched my own babies suffer through it, wishing I could assure them it would be okay, unable to offer more than ice, teething rings and occasionally rubbing their gums with my finger to help ease their pain. And I knew nothing was going to stop my need for Liam any more than the tooth can stop itself from pushing through the baby's gums. The baby knows innately that it won't die and that when the process is over, what it gains is a new tooth. But shit, I didn't know anything except that Liam said he loved me and I wanted—no, I needed—to know he needed me, too. I needed to know whether I was falling down Alice's Rabbit Hole by myself.

I steadied myself and walked out of the bathroom. My palms were sweaty and there was an intense sensation of heat rushing up the back of my neck and around my ears as though I had a fever. As if all this weren't bad enough, I couldn't get my mind to shut up. Maybe Liam's silence was because someone else had gotten his attention. If that were the case, so be it, I told myself. No intercessor would ever be a match for the girl who'd known him since we were sixteen. It didn't matter what paths our lives took after high school or how many marriages or how many children we had between us. Something had me fully convinced now that it didn't matter what the earthly circumstances or moral dictates were. Ours was a love that existed long ago, existed now, and would always exist.

But what if someone else really had begun to occupy Liam's thoughts because he was bored with me? It wasn't his wife. Of that, I was certain. But some other female, someone new? No doubt, it had started the same way it had started with me. Light conversation, occasional texting. Now, he wanted to know everything there was to know about this woman. He'd be witty and charming and make her laugh. He'd talk to her about connectedness and the universe and how she takes his breath away with her eyes or her smile or her walk. And soon she'd find the attention irresistible and thoughts of him would fill her every waking moment. Next, he'd share music with her. Oh, God, don't let him share music with her. My hand catapulted over my mouth, but not because I had to throw up again. It was the thought that sharing music with her would be the worst betrayal of all.

Chapter Ten

Love In An Elevator
Aerosmith, 1989

Garrett stepped off the subway into the chaotic crowd and climbed up the concrete stairs to the street. The air possessed the impenetrable humidity not too dissimilar from Toronto's on some days. Another three blocks and he would be able to retreat inside the American Museum of Natural History where he could escape the heat. He was accustomed to tourists but never before had he lived among so many of them. There was a vivid memory of a visit to New York City when he was five years old, when everything he craved to see was too far above his height level to get a glimpse, and because he had gotten too big to sit on top of his father's shoulders, he spent most of the excursions craning his head upward to see. It was hardly fair for such a little boy to have to count a sore neck among his summer vacation souvenirs, but that's the only thing he recalled bringing back from the trip. In actuality, it had most likely been mid-fall, not summer, because his father had no doubt strategically scheduled the visit during cooler weather. James McKinnon was a magnetic, highly educated, intensely driven individual who left very little to chance. He came from strong Celtic roots that dictated hard work as the basis for a successful life, and the loyalty of a loving wife and obedient children as the very least of the fruits of that labor.

Garrett had avoided the details when he told his father he was moving to New York City. It wasn't that his dad hadn't approved of Nicole, quite the opposite. Garrett had seen a twinkle in the old man's eye the first time his family met her, followed by one of those looks—in his piercing blue eyes that were an exact duplicate of Garrett's—between fathers and sons that need no words. It wasn't a look that portended Nicole was 'the one,' but Garrett could tell his father saw an undeniable bond between his son and this particular female that would not be easily severed. On the one hand, he would have cautioned Garrett about leaving Canada—and a secure job— to go live with Nicole. On the other hand, Garrett and his brothers always had their dad's blessing to go out into the world and make their own choices, "especially while you're young!" their father would say.

As he approached the entrance to the Hayden Planetarium, Garrett spotted Nicole. Whenever he had misgivings about his lukewarm love affair with New York, seeing her face made everything right. The only blemish in the picture was the excruciating pain developing from a blister on his right heel that had been made worse by the last several blocks' walk. But just like every other unpleasant thing he encountered, Nicole always had a way of making him forget about it, at least for the moment.

He gave Nicole the firm squeeze he always gave her the instant they saw each other, and then grabbed her hand as they quickly moved through the turn-style beneath the sign that said *Members*. Garrett loved the planetarium and all things that held mysteries beyond the atmosphere immediately surrounding him. The annual fee to join was not cheap for a twenty-four year old living in New York City earning a modest wage, but for Garrett it was an investment as significant as buying one's first house. He spent a lot of time here, taking in everything there was to see, always the first in line at the newest exhibit. But today he steered Nicole past everything without stopping.

"Where are we going?" she asked.

"You'll see."

In another minute they were nowhere near the museum crowd and wound up in an empty hallway that felt curiously as though it were for staff only. They turned down another hallway and discovered—well, *she* discovered, because Garrett appeared to already know exactly where he was going—a small elevator. He pushed the call button.

"What are we doing?" Nicole inquired.

"Shh," Garrett said.

The elevator door opened and a uniformed docent stepped out.

"Hey! You're not supposed to be—," the man barked as Garrett shoved past him, pulling Nicole with him into the empty elevator. Garrett hit the Close Door button, and then pushed '3.'

"Thanks! We'll send it back down," Garrett shouted back through the swiftly narrowing crack of the elevator door. Once the two were inside, Nicole turned to him wide-eyed.

"Are you crazy?" she said, suppressing a giggle.

"Why do you ask questions you know the answers to?" quipped Garrett.

He pushed the Emergency Stop button and the elevator halted with a thud. At the instant Nicole's brain registered what was going on, Garrett kissed her firmly on the mouth. She had known he was up to something, but she never thought he'd try to have sex with her in the elevator inside the planetarium! Because they had a chemistry that made it impossible for her to resist him, her arms slipped around his neck, giving in to the kiss. It was the kind of kiss that specifically revealed where it would lead. Not the playful kind, but the kind with a declaration of intent, and the thrill of it made her entire body more aware of the heat emanating from his.

With his parted lips he caressed the side of her neck and she grew limp from the sensation as the steady increase of pressure of his body against hers caused a delicate moan to escape her throat. His hands found the hem of her skirt—the short, flowy, lavender one that caught his eye when she put it on this morning and remained on his mind all day—and raised it above her hips. He slid his hand inside her panties. She grabbed a fistful of his cotton shirt and tugged it upward to get it out of his jeans while her other hand groped for his belt buckle.

What sounded like muffled voices could be heard outside the elevator.

"What if we get in trouble?" Nicole whispered breathlessly.

"Let's hope…" Garrett uttered.

His pants were open now and with only the wall of the elevator against her back and Garrett's body to hold her up, Nicole reached down and guided him inside her. Their passion launched them to a mindless place where everything that existed outside the unleashed chemistry between them, vanished. When Garrett climaxed, Nicole sealed her hand over his mouth for fear he'd be heard. With his pelvis still pressed against hers, she felt his hand make its way between her thighs and his skillful fingers brought her to an orgasm that caused her to collapse in his arms, and send them both sinking slowly to the floor.

The sound of Nicole's heavy panting filled the elevator. Her eyes were closed and she delighted in the touch of Garrett's skin. She felt his breath as he whispered in her ear.

"Well, that's a smile if I ever saw one."

"Bragger."

"Not bragging," Garrett said. "Just loving the look on your face."

"I just thought of something," Nicole said.

"That we need to fix our clothes?"

"No. Well, that, too. But I never heard an alarm or anything."

"You know, you're right. I didn't either."

"Isn't an alarm supposed to go off when you stop the elevator?"

"I don't know. But you certainly got my alarm off, that's for sure."

They climbed up from the floor. Once they made themselves presentable, Garrett released the emergency stop button and pushed '1'.

Afraid that something about them would expose their deed, they made their way back toward the common area of the planetarium like a couple of five year olds who had stolen a treat from the cookie jar. They stared straight ahead, and encountered a museum employee, as wide as she was tall, approaching from the opposite direction.

"This area is for employees only," the woman announced.

Garrett and Nicole offered up a response at the same time, tripping over each other's speech.

"Oh, um, we got lost. But we kind of know where we are, now. The exit's this way, right?" Nicole responded, using her acting skills.

"Yes," the woman answered with a monotone air of suspicion.

"Actually we're looking for the laser show," said Garrett.

Nicole looked at him. "We are?"

"Yeah," Garrett adjusted smoothly. "Can you tell us how to get to it?"

"You were looking for the laser show and ended up all the way back here?" the woman said, her fixed gaze burning into the two suspects.

"Mm-hm," Nicole nodded.

"Do I look stupid?" the woman asked.

"Oh my goodness, no, not at all!" Nicole replied.

Their interrogator took a deep breath and shook her head back and forth. "Keep down this hallway. In a minute it'll dump you out at the meteor exhibit. You'll see some stairs on the left. The laser show is down those stairs and straight ahead."

"Thank you so much," Garrett gushed. He grabbed Nicole's hand again. "We better hurry."

"Wait—so you really *do* want to see the laser show?" she asked when they were out of earshot of the woman.

"Yeah."

"I thought you were just—"

"Making it up?"

"Yeah."

"Nope. Have you heard about it?"

"No."

Garrett smiled. "Then you're in for a treat."

"I thought… we already had our… treat," Nicole replied in her best Marilyn Monroe tone of voice.

"That wasn't a treat," Garrett said, throwing his arm around her. "That was a premeditated, beautifully executed, visit to heaven and back," he declared, planting a loud series of kisses on Nicole's cheek, sending her into a cascade of giggles. "This, on the other hand, will be nothing like you've ever seen before. Or heard. All to Pink Floyd."

"You've already seen it?"

"Yeah. Prepare to be amazed."

A dense crowd of tourists in front of the meteor exhibit blocked the path to the lower level staircase. Garrett managed to maneuver through.

"Oh my God!" someone shouted. "Aren't you that actress from that soap opera, 'Don't Look Back?'"

"Nope, it's not her!" Garrett yelled towards the voice, as he and his girlfriend disappeared quickly down the stairs to their next adventure.

Chapter Eleven

Maybe I'm Amazed
Paul McCartney, 1970

Lisa doesn't just love him, she *needs* him. I'm not seeing the vulnerability, like—we need to wonder what would happen to her if he left. We need to think she can't live without him. Right now it's coming across like you're just happy to have him around, you know what I mean?"

Nicole always dreaded Tim's notes. Not because he wasn't a good director, but because she always believed that if nothing else, she was an emotional person, and it made her angry that she couldn't always trust those emotions to come through when she needed them to. It was a frustration all actors faced from time to time. Tim, however, never seemed to have any trouble emoting, on or off the stage. Nicole and a few of the cast members from the show had seen him perform on Broadway. He was not only a gifted actor, he was ruggedly handsome with thick, dark, chin-length hair that framed a face of strongly chiseled features most likely of Mediterranean origin, attached to a Herculean build that came from his parents, not Gold's Gym. In conversation, he looked everywhere but directly at you, except now and then to punctuate his sentences. This wasn't because he was shy, but because he was one of those artists on steroids who was constantly stimulated by spontaneous streams of creative ideas.

"You're not getting that I need him?" Nicole asked. It was a stupid question. If just once in her life she would prove her second grade teacher wrong and actually take criticism well.

"No. Otherwise I wouldn't be telling you."

"Okay," as Nicole crossed her arms over her chest. Great—the arms are crossed, so the mind is closed, Tim thought.

"Don't get upset, just fix it."

"I'm not upset," Nicole insisted.

"Okay. Then, you know what I'm talking about, right?"

"Yes."

"In this relationship, the need is as strong as the love. Maybe, even stronger. Otherwise there's no risk. We don't care. It's boring. But that doesn't mean she's obsessed, either. It's not obsession," Tim explained, creating less clarity the more he talked.

"Okay," Nicole nodded.

"Think about your relationship with Garrett. You love him?"

"Of course."

"You need him?"

"Well… yeah."

"See, you hesitated!"

"No, I didn't!"

"Yes, you did! You said 'of course' you love him, and then I asked if you needed him and you said, 'well, yeah.' Very different. That's what's wrong. Lisa loves Jason. I get that. You have no trouble conveying that. Does Lisa need Jason? I don't know because you're doing 'well, yeah.' Find out what needing Garrett feels like. And show me that at the next rehearsal."

Tim marched back towards the stage. Nicole sauntered into her dressing room. She closed the door behind her and lowered herself onto the stool in front of the mirror. For a couple minutes she stared at the girl looking back at her. She was pretty certain she knew her, but there were days, like today, that she wasn't sure. Perhaps it was closer to the truth to say she knew her all too well but wasn't always sure she wanted to *be* her. The girl in the mirror shared all Nicole's shortcomings but rarely offered any productive tips for improvement. Where was the help in that? Didn't she know that Nicole longed to surrender to love? Why was she afraid to? No one knew her like Garrett did. No one would ever love her the way Garrett would. Her heart stopped the first time he looked at her and from that point on, her heart broke every time he left the room. Nicole's mind drifted to a time she and Garrett were still living in different cities and she hadn't been able to reach him for two days.

***

It was a Saturday. She was curled up in a ball in the middle of her sofa bed, arms wrapped around her knees. The storm outside was sending the rain down in buckets as it had been doing continuously since the night before, making Nicole content to stay inside and study Monday's script. As always, when it rained, she placed a towel on the floor to catch the leak in the window casing on the other side of the apartment. The wall clock she'd fallen in love with at a flea market announced that it had been seven hours since she'd left Garrett a message. The clock's rhythmic ticking created a duet with the tapping of each drop of water that descended on the nearly soaked surface of the towel below. It was odd that Nicole hadn't heard from him, and probably nothing to be concerned about. But in the past twenty hours, there'd been no response from the two messages she'd left.

"Hey, it's me. What are you doing? Call me back. Love you."

That was at eight last night. She'd stayed up as late as possible hoping she would hear back from him, but finally drifted off to sleep. At nine o'clock this morning, she called again. Unlike Nicole, Garrett was an early riser and would have already been up for at least a couple hours by then. But again, there was no answer. She left another message.

"Okay. Where in the world are you?"

The connection she and Garrett had to each other had always possessed some strange life force of its own and when weakened, Nicole was changed. It was a bond like some invisible cord that connected the two of them together. And right now, that cord was being stretched and twisted and no amount of looking around her apartment for him was going to conjure Garrett's presence. She refused to stare at the phone, but found herself doing it anyway. She refused to be that 'needy, clingy' girlfriend she promised herself she would never turn into. It was so 'high school.' In fact, Nicole regretted there was no fairy godmother back in high school that would appear out of nowhere to tell the 'needy, clingy' girlfriends that their attitude may as well be a pillow held over their boyfriends' faces, and rid them of their obnoxious behavior. Perhaps she shouldn't have judged those girls so harshly. After all, none of them had a Garrett McKinnon at their side— literally, and in spirit—at all times, in all places, who adored them and balanced them and anchored them. It was a special kind of bond, a Romeo and Juliet type of connection that Nicole could have explained to Shakespeare, himself, had he required inspiration for his story.

She got up from the sofa bed and paced while running her lines out loud. She paced for the rest of the afternoon and into the evening, stopping only to make a glass of iced tea, never changed out of her PJs, and never went down to check the mail. Her palms were sweaty and her stomach nauseous. She felt a sensation of heat shoot up her neck, and through her ears. At one point, she felt as if she couldn't breathe, and found herself flying across the room to force open that leaky window for a deep breath of damp air. This asthmatic scare was followed by a rapid trip to the bathroom where she was certain she was going to throw up. She gave the sink faucet an abrupt twist too far, creating a gush of water that went everywhere when she placed the corner of a hand towel under it. The result was an ice cold shower that sprayed Nicole and a half dozen other items in the bathroom in the process. Gripping the edge of the counter in an effort to steady herself over the toilet, she heard the phone ring. Holding the towel to her mouth, she raced from the bathroom to get it.

"Hello?"

"Hey, it's me. I slept over at Nonie's house last night after I went to the hospital to see her. Mum and Dad are with her now, so I came home. You okay?"

Nicole's heart stabilized. Her stomach settled. And the temperature in her face returned to normal.

Chapter Twelve

(You Make Me Feel Like) A Natural Woman
Aretha Franklin, 1967

This new territory—intimate conversations with a man who wasn't my husband—was totally manageable, I thought. I was filling whatever void Liam needed me to fill, and in return I loved the attention. What had started as occasionally touching base to say "hi," was turning into conversations that took place every day, first thing in the morning, last thing at night. I grew to anticipate hearing from him. I knew he anticipated it, too.

***

MIRANDA: Hi, handsome.

LIAM: Hi, gorgeous.

MIRANDA: Sorry, I know it's late there.

LIAM: Don't be sorry.

MIRANDA: Why are you still up?

LIAM: Waiting to hear from you.

MIRANDA: I feel a little bad that I'm keeping you
awake. You can say good-night to me
anytime. I won't mind.

LIAM: But I don't want to.

MIRANDA: Okay. But, I'll warn you, I could talk
forever.

LIAM: I love hearing everything on your mind.

MIRANDA: You're sweet.

LIAM: It's true.

MIRANDA: And I tend to ramble.

LIAM: I love it when you ramble.

MIRANDA: In fact, there are probably some men who
would say I've actually put them to sleep
with my rambling.

LIAM: Then they were fools.

MIRANDA: You think?

LIAM: Yes.

MIRANDA: You don't think they were probably just tired?

LIAM: If they were just tired as in sleepy, I might cut them a little slack. If they were tired of hearing you talk, they should have come up with more creative ways to stop you from talking.

MIRANDA: Oh dear. I like the way you think.

LIAM: I like the way I think, too. Would you like to hear the ways I'd stop you from talking?

MIRANDA: Um… okay.

LIAM: I promise I won't ask you what you're wearing.

MIRANDA: You don't wanna know what I'm wearing? LOL.

LIAM: Not interested.

MIRANDA: Too cliché?

LIAM: I'd rather imagine that you're not wearing anything.

MIRANDA: And I took you for the romantic, slow,

build up type.

LIAM: Oh, I am. But what are you wearing is
a game. The idea of savoring every inch
of your naked body is not a game to me.
LIAM: Are you still there?

MIRANDA: Yes.

LIAM: You got quiet.

MIRANDA: Just trying to recover from your comment.

LIAM: About having your body all to myself?

MIRANDA: Yes. Well, that's not exactly how you put it,
but, yes.

LIAM: Sorry, I didn't mean to offend you. I have
the utmost respect for you. I always have.

MIRANDA: No, it's okay. It's just—it made me
go weak all over, that's all.

LIAM: Oh. Then that's a good thing, I guess.

MIRANDA: Makes me wanna hear more.

LIAM: Another time.

MIRANDA: Are you teasing me, now?

LIAM: Maybe just a little.

MIRANDA: That's not fair!

LIAM: Sure, it is. I've ignited your imagination.
For now, I'm a happy man.

MIRANDA: That's all it takes to make you happy?

LIAM: I said, for now.

MIRANDA: I see. Well, you have, indeed, ignited my
imagination, Liam Kincaid.

LIAM: Oh, good. Cuz I'm guessing yours is pretty
unlimited.

MIRANDA: You think so?

LIAM: Oh, I'd bet on it.

MIRANDA: Why's that?

LIAM: First of all, you're a writer. Second,
you're a woman in love.

MIRANDA: Have me all figured out, do you?
LIAM: Well, I already know you're a writer. Fully comprehending the woman could
take another thousand years.

MIRANDA: Didn't your mother teach you patience?

LIAM: Yes. But she also taught me to never try
to comprehend a woman because it
would take me a thousand years.

MIRANDA: LOL. She was right.

LIAM: Indeed, she was.
MIRANDA: Sigh… I wonder if you know
the effect you're starting to have on me.

LIAM: I imagine it's the same as the effect you
have on me.

MIRANDA: Do I really?

LIAM: Of course.

MIRANDA: You know something?

LIAM: Tell me.

MIRANDA: I've never in my life called a man
"baby."

LIAM: That makes me smile. Among other
physical responses.

MIRANDA: I'm being serious!

LIAM: So am I!

MIRANDA: There've been men who've been my
sweetheart, honey, darling, maybe.
But with you, baby seems to roll off my
tongue so easily. I don't know why.

LIAM: Does it matter why?

MIRANDA: No.

LIAM: You over think things.

MIRANDA: Guilty as charged.

LIAM: Just be glad.

MIRANDA: That you're the only man I've ever called
baby?

LIAM: Yes. I certainly am.

MIRANDA: Certainly glad? Or certainly my baby?

LIAM: Both.

MIRANDA: You really should go to sleep.

LIAM: I have another hour or so at the piano.

MIRANDA: Still working on that song you told me about?

LIAM: Yep. It's coming along slowly. My version is a little simpler than the original. It's one of the most beautiful pieces of music ever written in my opinion. I'll send you a recording of it. Prepare to be moved.

***

He was talking about Pat Metheny's *September 15*. I was familiar with the contemporary jazz guitarist, popular for his innovative use of the synthesizer, but I'd never heard the song before. Nor had I ever heard anything like it. The piece was composer Lyle Mays' tribute to the late, great American jazz composer and pianist Bill Evans, who died on September 15, 1980. From the first note, I was drawn in, frozen in some part of time, in some far off place, yet strangely present at the same time. The tones were melancholy but joyful, sorrowful but healing, evoking almost a celebration of everything that could go wrong in a life, woven with some mysterious sweetness that reached down inside of me and touched me at my core. I sobbed uncontrollably the first time I heard it, unsure if I could stop, but half way through the song there was a lifting, a rescuing from somewhere in the depths of one's sadness to a place of hope and gratitude and love.

It was a musical experience not just of emotions but of colors and of movement. If I listened to it with my eyes closed, I saw electric waves of turquoise and chartreuse, iridescent streams of goldenrod and flashes of rose-petal-pink. There was a spinning sensation that sent me flying, and then next I was floating to the surface of— something—where I felt cleansed when I reached the top. It would be several months before I could listen to the first twelve measures without starting to cry. But soon twelve measures became sixteen, sixteen became twenty, and twenty grew into twenty-four before the powerful emotional tug was too great to hold back tears. And it would be an eternity before I would ever hear it without thinking of Liam.

***

The songs Liam sent me were like gifts at Christmas time. They were the most beautiful of seashells unearthed from the sand by the ocean waves. They were the spectacular Crown Jewels displayed behind the glass cases inside the Tower of London. On some days, they were simply food for my soul. On other days, one of them could open a well of emotion in me so deep that I would cry incessantly. Sometimes, they spoke in a whisper. Sometimes, they shouted. There were ones with messages straight from his heart that could cause me to toss and turn for hours, or put me to sleep like a lullaby, if that's what he intended. Liam's lifelong love affair with music taught him at an early age that it could tell a story or simply serve as punctuation at the end of our thoughts. It could be the glue that holds together whatever is fragmented. It could touch us somewhere inside and literally

84

save us from ourselves. Music became wrapped around our relationship and lived at the center of it at the same time. It was heart and also blood. It flowed and poured and oozed into the cracks. If he thought a piece was a work of genius, I tried to listen for its intricacies. If he wanted it to soothe me or elate me, it did. If he wanted me to hear *I love you* in it, I would.

His music became my music.

Chapter Thirteen

Love You Inside Out
The Bee Gees, 1979

The plane touched down at Toronto's Pearson International. Nicole gave up counting the times she'd made this trip over the last few years. Since Garrett moved to New York, she was thankful that the days of flying back and forth to see him were over, but this particular week he was in Canada because his grandmother only had a few days to live and James wanted Garrett home so the family could be together. It was a crazy—somewhat selfish—idea, she thought, surprising him out of the blue this way, but she wanted to tell him in person about her Emmy nomination. She was still in shock over it herself, and to see the look on Garrett's face when she told him she was nominated would be second only to the sweetness of receiving the award itself.

Maybe the news would cheer him up and the sight of her would be a pleasant distraction during this difficult time. Nicole remembered when she lost her own grandmother during her sophomore year in college. Beatrice, or 'Mama,' as she was called, was a smart, beautiful, spit-fire of a woman. Mama had come to stay with them for the summer and when she left Wishton to go home, she told Nicole, "Give Mama a hug. You're not going to see me anymore." She passed away three months later, and took a part of Nicole with her that would be missing for years to come.

There was no answer when Nicole rang the buzzer to Garrett's building, so she used the key card she still had to his place and took the elevator up to the third floor. Her salary from the soap was enough to cover their apartment in New York, so Garrett kept the loft in Liberty Village in case he ever needed it. When Nicole heard the funky, gyrating strains of the Bee Gees' *Love You Inside and Out* coming from the other side of the door, a smile came across her face. It was one of her favorite songs, and she was reminded of the show's season kick-off party when she'd requested it from the DJ. When the song started, Nicole took Garrett's hand and pulled him onto the dance floor. The two of them moved to the rhythm, their love for each other so obvious and so sweet, the entire cast and crew cleared the floor and watched them as they danced, everyone clapping to the beat. Garrett surrendered to his discomfort at being the center of attention and became, instead, caught up in the magic of it all. Nicole would never forget the look on his face and how wonderful she felt.

The music inside the loft was so loud that Garrett would never hear the doorbell, let alone a knock on the door, so Nicole let herself in. It had been a while since she'd felt the familiarity of this apartment and she was surprised to discover how nice it was to be in a space belonging only to him. But Garrett wasn't there. Had he suddenly run out and left the music blaring? She turned down the stereo. Now that it was quieter, she could hear the sound of the shower. *That explains it*, she thought. No wonder she couldn't find him. Just as her mouth was about to call out, "Garrett," Nicole heard a giggle coming from the bathroom. It was a female giggle. Then the female giggle was followed by the sound of Garrett talking. It was the first time Nicole hoped she was mistaking someone else's voice for Garrett's. But she wasn't. She knew his voice like she knew his laugh, and the way he walked, and the exact way he put mustard on his turkey sandwiches.

That doesn't make sense, Nicole thought. *The only female here is me.*

Unless there's another female here, her brain replied.

Okay. That's fine. Who said he can't have female friends?

Of course, he can. But in the bathroom with him? In the shower?

Nicole grew nauseous and the nausea made her weak. She steadied her legs beneath her and summoned the part of her that serves up the perfect dose of courage when a woman needs it. She marched across the room and stood in the slightly opened doorway of the bathroom. The picture she encountered registered with the cerebrum of her brain but did so without any logic to support it.

The roar of the water gushing from the shower head diminished to virtual silence, while the two naked figures standing beneath it were plainly visible through the fine layer of steam that coated the surface of the clear plastic curtain. Nicole struggled to comprehend Garrett's arms wrapped around the curvaceous frame that wasn't Nicole's, one of the cheeks of its slippery wet derriere firmly in Garrett's hand. But Garrett, whose body was facing the bathroom door, had no trouble at all comprehending that Nicole was suddenly standing there. He let go of the sudsy visitor and jumped out of the shower.

"Nicole!"

Garrett's wet bare feet raced through the loft. But the only trace of the girl he'd loved since they were sixteen was the open door to the apartment where she'd dashed out as fast as she could. He looked down the hall, but Nicole was gone.

The sudsy visitor, still somewhat damp and dressed only in an over-sized sweatshirt and panties, emerged from the bathroom to find Garrett banging his fist against the door frame.

"I'm sorry," she whispered.

Garrett closed the door and strolled over to a pile of clothes in the chair and traded the towel around his waist for a pair of jeans. The phone rang. Then rang again. Then rang a third time.

"Are you going to get that?" the sudsy visitor asked.

"They can leave a message," Garrett mumbled, and sank down onto the sofa with his head in his hands.

Another ring. The tape machine picked up.

"Hey, this is Garrett. Thomas Edison said 'to invent, you need a good imagination and a pile of junk.' So at the beep leave me a message on this pile of junk."

"Garrett, it's your father. Just wanted you to know Nonie's gone. She passed away about an hour ago. No need for you to drive over till the morning, son. Give us a call when you get this."

Garrett looked in the direction of the phone. He closed his eyes and let out a long sigh. He thought of how he could always count on one of Nonie's hugs whenever he was sad, or whenever he was hurt, or whenever the trouble he was in was really his own fault. When he was little, Nonie would cup his chubby-cheeked face in her velvet palms, and then give him the most loving, suffocating hug he ever knew. He wished she were there to hug him that way now. But she wasn't, and she never would be again.

Sudsy Visitor wasn't sure what to say in light of the events of the last several minutes, and offered simply, "Do you want me to go?"

"It's just really been a crazy night. I kind of need to be alone, sorry," Garrett said.

"It's okay."

She said nothing as she finished getting dressed, not wanting to increase the awkwardness in the room with any more conversation.

She was developing strong feelings for the blue-eyed Canadian-turned-New-Yorker with the actress girlfriend, and although they had been together only one other time before tonight, she hoped he was starting to feel the same way about her. The coincidence that they met in New York and were both from Canada was interesting, though not unusual. She was painfully shy and he'd been so charming every morning when he came into the coffee shop where she worked, that soon he'd gotten her to open up about the classes she was taking at NYU. One of them was Phys-UA-50 (Astrophysics) and though Garrett was not the TA for that particular course, she was thrilled there was a topic they shared a major interest in, and even more thrilled when he offered her the spare ticket he had to the symphony. When she invited him to stay over at her place after the concert, she prayed it would be more than just a one night stand. But if that's all it turned out to be, she thought, it was okay, because there was something about being in his arms just for one night that made her loneliness disappear.

Regrettably, she didn't hear from him for a few weeks after that. Then, about a month ago, he came into the coffee shop again. He was just as warm and funny as always, and, of course, the perfect gentleman. She had struggled to conceal her joy at seeing him again. She had been a silly little fool, after all. She told him she was moving back to Canada and that whenever he was back for a visit, perhaps they could get a double-double. That's what today had been about. But just like the night of the symphony, the evening had developed into far more. And added to everything else that had just happened, was the paralyzing fear that her period was late.

Chapter Fourteen

One Last Cry
Brian McKnight, 1992

If the seventh application of ice failed to take down the swelling from her eyes, Nicole wasn't sure how they'd be able to put her on tape today. She hadn't cried on the flight home and she hadn't cried in the cab on the way from the airport. In fact, she was getting fairly good at managing her emotions in public. Unfortunately, that didn't keep folks from chit chatting about her.

"How long do you think she's going to sit there?" the stewardess asked her coworker.

"I don't know."

"Should we wake her up?"

"She's not asleep."

"She's not? Are you sure?"

"She's been staring out the window the whole flight, like she's in a trance or something. Nothing to see out there now but concrete. When I asked her if she wanted something to drink, I could've sworn she looked at me, but she acted like she didn't hear me."

"Do you think she's okay?"

"Okay or not, she's gotta get off the plane." The stewardess walked down the aisle to the seat where Nicole was wrapped up to her chin with a blanket.

"I'm going," Nicole announced softly, still gazing out the window.

"I'm sorry," the flight attendant answered.

Nicole robotically removed the blanket and placed it on the seat next to her.

"Wait—you're Nicole Martin, right?" the attendant asked.

Nicole nodded 'yes' and reached for the carry-on she'd brought on board.

"Oh my gosh, I love you in Don't Look Back! It's my favorite soap!"

"Thanks." Nicole forced a smile and headed down the aisle to the front of the aircraft.

"If you don't mind my asking, are you okay? Can I get you some water or something, for the road?"

"No, thanks."

"You just—look like you just lost your best friend or something."

Nicole continued walking and kept her head down so the stewardess wouldn't see her face. When she got halfway through the empty exit tunnel where no one could hear, she uttered, "Yeah... you could say that."

Once inside the brownstone and the floodgates were open, Nicole couldn't stop crying. Had she ever cried this much? Maybe when she was five or six years old? Or maybe when Pierre, the family's cocker spaniel, ran away when Nicole was eleven? The only other time she could remember crying this much, was that winter's day in Wishton when Garrett told her he was moving away. That was seven years ago. A lot had happened since then. Graduation from high school and then college, a TV contract right after that, leaving the comfort of a small town for the harshness of Pittsburgh, leaving Pittsburgh for the glitter of New York. It was a lot of adjusting for a girl in her early 20s, and it had all happened very fast. The only constant, the only thing that remained the same throughout everything her young life was throwing at her, was Garrett.

This thing that happened yesterday, this fly in the ointment—and it was a pretty big fly—she hoped was no more than that. Without a doubt, Garrett would have an explanation. It was going to boil down to someone he met at a party the other night and perhaps he'd had a little too much to drink and he couldn't get rid of her. Somehow they ended up in the… shower together. If only she could erase the image from her mind. Of course, that was better than walking in on them in the middle of—oh, God—what if they had done it? To assume otherwise was just naive. Nicole wished with all her heart she could be naive about this. She'd do anything to be back in junior high school when boys were no more than mysterious entities to whisper about among your girlfriends. But when it came time to talk to Garrett about what happened last night, it wasn't going to feel like they were back in junior high school. Hearing what Garrett had to say was going to be like sitting in the dentist's chair having to endure the entire painful process until it was over. The sun rose and set in his eyes. The light inside her came from inside of him. Why had he gone and ruined it all?

The last soggy washcloth-full of ice sent a shiver up Nicole's wrist and through her body. The phone rang. It was too early for it to be Rob, the stage manager from the show. There was still a little time left before he'd be calling to see if she was running late. On the sixth ring, the tape machine picked up.

"Hi, it's Nicole. Sorry I missed your call. Please leave a message at the sound of the tone and I'll get back to you as soon as possible. Thanks."

"Nicole, pick up…"

Nicole squeezed her eyes shut. The person on the line was not her Garrett. He had Garrett's voice, Garrett's gentle strength, but this guy was somebody she didn't know.

"I know you're there, Nicky. You're never out the door this early… Dammit, Nicole! We have to talk about this. Why won't you talk to me?"

She opened her swollen eyes just enough to focus a halfhearted gaze that rested on the floor.

"Okay. Well. I'm staying here till after the funeral next week, and then I'll be home. If you haven't changed the locks. You gotta talk to me at some point, Nicole. I love you. Bye."

The machine clicked off.

That was the fourth message from Garrett since last night. The first was waiting for her when she got home. Understandably, he was upset and just said to please call him as soon as she got in. She didn't. When he called back the second time, he said he wanted her to know Grandma

Nonie had passed. Although it was expected, Nicole's heart broke upon hearing the news. Nonie was a sweet, delightful little wisp of a woman. Nicole had only met her once, and it had been instant mutual adoration. The third call had come in the middle of the night. She didn't recall exactly what Garrett had said or how long the message was, because the only thing she'd been able to hear through her own sobs was simply, "Nicole…"

The clock on the nightstand warned that if she was going to go to work, she'd better get moving. Then it occurred to her that none of Garrett's messages said anything like *it wasn't what you think* or *it didn't mean anything*. The thought that Garrett might actually have a relationship with Sudsy Visitor made Nicole feel sick. He had never given her a reason not to trust him. He had never given her a reason to imagine what the world would be like if he fell in love with someone else. She didn't know what to do except close her eyes and pull the covers over her head. Hopefully by the time Rob called, she'd be nearly comatose from physical and emotional exhaustion. She couldn't feel guilty about ignoring the phone if she never heard it.

Chapter Fifteen

Goin' Out of My Head
Queen Latifah, 1998

"**N**ext. Next!… Ma'am?"
It seemed like the voice was directed at me, but I couldn't be sure. The last thing I remembered was there had been two people in front of me in the line, and the line was in the bank. I knew that for sure because no matter how cozy and inviting banks tried to design their interiors, as far as I was concerned, they were nothing more than cold and sterile and untrustworthy dwellings dedicated to proving their place for your funds was superior to the space underneath your mattress. I was already frustrated that I actually had to go *inside* the bank today instead of just to the ATM outside. I couldn't recall when the two individuals in front of me disappeared, because I was still completely lost in the experience from last night.

I'd talked to Liam until two o'clock in the morning. When I told him goodnight, and turned out the light, that's when it all began. It wasn't a dream because I was still awake. It wasn't a vision because there was no picture of anything in my mind. Some may have called it a ghost, but it felt human. The human was a *he* and my body knew exactly who *he* was. He was on top of me, beneath me, behind me, over me. I could feel him, his weight, his breath, his lips, his pelvis, his… I could feel *all* of it. I was grabbing and clutching and hanging onto him for dear life. I was trembling and gasping and wanting it to last forever.

So, you had a fantasy, I thought. *What's the big deal?*

But *fantasy* didn't seem to be the right word for this dream-vision-thing I'd experienced. It had a life of its own, navigated by something outside my imagination. It hadn't been my thoughts that prevented me from sleeping, but a presence. Every time I drifted back to sleep, he was back again. If it was true what Liam believed about our ability to exist on other realms, there was no doubt in my mind that he was in my bed last night. Although just three seconds of the entire replay were enough to launch my body into a state of arousal, the greater mystery shoved its way to the forefront of my mind: which Liam, the one from my past, my present, or even another lifetime, had visited me? And how long could I deny they were one person?

***

After I maneuvered through the bank and back to my car, the next stop was the grocery store, another errand in a long list of obligations on my day off. It wasn't that I didn't appreciate having a day off, I just hated that it was no different from any other day in another year of another dead-end job that did nothing to serve my creative self. Hell, it was worse than not serving my creative self. It was actually killing my creative self. The thought took me back to a poem I'd written years ago entitled, 'Wrong Room.' It was all about how ending up in the wrong place in your life was similar to ending up in the wrong room on the first day of elementary school, and the feelings of shame, humiliation and awkwardness that accompanied the mistake. It was a very short poem yet all I could remember of it was the last line: *A clown who will die if he cannot dance for the children.*

I pulled into our cul-de-sac, still feeling Liam all over my body, grateful that the next chore of putting away the groceries would be a mindless one. Back in the house, I threw my keys on the kitchen counter. Not a soul was home to help me unload the groceries from the car—probably a good thing, I needed to decompress. I could never manage to carry more than one bag of groceries at a time, but the task was made more difficult today by the weakness in my knees left by last night's fantasy. I wanted to stop right where I was and relive the entire thing again, but the brown paper bags, nine in all, sat gawking at me, begging to be emptied.

Why didn't I know where to start? Frozen foods, first. It was basic. Why did I have to think it through? Why did I suddenly feel like an alien in my own kitchen who had no idea what to do with these various items lined up in identical paper containers? It wasn't a bizarre memory lapse. It was that it was there, again, the feeling of Liam's breath on the back of my neck. *Put your big girl panties on and snap out of it*, a voice said. *Okay.* I'd basked long enough in the feeling of making love to Liam, invented or not, and needed to get back to mundane reality. Was that *panties* I'd heard the voice say? I'd felt him pull them off me with one hand while he held my body tightly against his own. How was I ever going to get through this afternoon? All I wanted was the night to come so I could go to bed and conjure Liam again.

But Liam wasn't really with me last night. And he wasn't going to be with me tonight, either. And I was angry. I slammed the refrigerator door and banged the cupboards in frustration. A slam for my career. Another slam for my marriage. A firm shove for my children, who, through no fault of their own, unknowingly tortured me daily by dangling the pending *empty nest* in my face. If *empty nest* had an image, I determined it would not be a mama sparrow sitting sadly at the edge of her vacated, perfectly woven bowl of broken twigs and frayed twine. It would be a cartoon of a middle aged woman holding a bleeding, Valentine-shaped heart in her hand, blood dripping through her fingers, and on her chest would be a hole in the shape of another Valentine-shaped heart, through which you could see all the way to the other side, like looking through a keyhole. The image always made me giggle. The giggling helped.

If there were any consolation for an empty-nesting mother, it was that her children couldn't know the pain inflicted by their separation from her, until, and unless, they had children of their own. 'The parent-child relationship is the only human relationship intended to grow towards separation,' a saying Neil and I always enjoyed quoting. Neil. Had our love making ever been the way I imagined it with Liam?

I tossed the last item from the afternoon's bounty, a package of provolone cheese, into the refrigerator and gave the door one more slam. Did Liam like provolone cheese? It wasn't fair the way he invaded my thoughts. There were days I saw his face everywhere. If I didn't see his face, I saw his name. If I didn't see his name, I saw his name inside words that had the same letters.

I leaned back against the counter, the cold edge of the granite pressing through my cotton Henley, closed my eyes, and surrendered the weight of my forehead into the heel of my hand in defeat.

What the hell is happening?

Wasn't this the very thing Liam told me not to do? Try to figure it out? But didn't he know there was this thing pulling me towards him through some space from which I felt powerless to return? And that this place where I found myself was starting to feel more like home, than home?

Bet he's not sitting somewhere a bewildered mess, I thought. *He's not tortured over this.*

Tortured or not, I still wanted to know exactly how he was doing at that moment. Was he having a good day? Or a rotten one? Was he happy? Sleepy? Grumpy? Dopey? Oh, God, I was naming the Seven Dwarfs! Had he gone grocery shopping, too? What had he bought? What would he have for dinner? Would he cook or would she—ughh, there it was—the fact that there was a *she*. My brain immediately deleted the word *she* from the line of questioning. Had he eaten lunch or had he skipped it to-day? And why did it feel so damn natural to want to know? I already knew plenty about him. I knew his favorite color and his favorite wine and his favorite kind of weather. But now, I wanted to know everything, just as he was starting to know everything about me. My likes, my dislikes, my wants, my needs, mostly because he had simply asked, and then simply listened. And that kind of attention from a man was intoxicating. Jesus, had we really missed out on an entire lifetime together?

I gave the stainless steel door a final slam for finding myself in love with the man who had gotten away.

***

I stormed out of the kitchen and did what I always did when I was overwhelmed with life's unanswered questions. I listened to my favorite music. This time it was *Stairway to Heaven* by guitarist Stanley Jordan, a version that Liam had sent me. I kicked off my Clarks thongs and collapsed onto our worn, dark chestnut leather sofa. A woman can have a love affair with a piece of furniture the way we can have a love affair with a particular pair of shoes, and I adored this couch from the moment I'd laid eyes on it years ago. There it was, handsome and beckoning, waiting for me in the back room of a home furnishings wholesale outlet on the edge of Santa Clarita. Who knows how long it had been yearning for us to meet?

Flat on my back, I pointed my toes and stretched them out as far as they could go, striving to make contact with the curved arm at the end of the couch. They couldn't reach. Perfect, I thought. With nothing touching the crown of my head, and nothing to hinder my feet, there was a sensation of complete freedom. I turned the volume on my earphones all the way up until the music suffocated the sound of my thoughts. I felt my body climb inside the melody and the strings of the guitar wrap around me like a cocoon. Over and over I played it, until the thoughts about the boy, turned man, turned soul mate, left me for a little while.

Chapter Sixteen

In Too Deep
Genesis, 1986

Nicole never understood the hype about Tavern on the Green. It was one of New York's most beautiful, iconic restaurants—beautiful and busy, like glamorous celebrities, many of whom frequented the place—but she always found it somewhat overrated. It was almost 11:30, still a few minutes before the lunch crowd. If this went quickly, she would be back to the studio before 1:00. She'd called ahead to ask for a table at the farthest end of the Central Park Room. It was the latest instruction from Jill, her publicist, for Nicole to remember that she was becoming increasingly recognizable in public and that her private life was becoming decreasingly private.

Being recognizable felt good most of the time, but it wasn't going to feel good this morning, so Nicole took Jill's advice and hoped that everybody in the restaurant would be far too self-absorbed in their own self-absorbed business to look around to see who else was self-absorbed in theirs. Nicole found some of Jill's concerns silly. After all, Nicole was just grateful to have a steady acting job. (When it's drilled into you, from the moment you express interest in the occupation, that being an actor is about starving, not working, the ability to make an actual living in the profession was not just considered gravy; it was white truffle cream sauce.) But Jill was the expert, and she told Nicole to be prepared for the Emmy nomination to skyrocket her career and send gazillions of dollars falling out of the sky into all of their pockets. *We'll see*, Nicole had thought. *Don't be so negative*, her mom's voice had replied (the same voice that had warned Nicole she would starve).

Garrett followed the deliberate gait of the hostess to a table that seemed to take the five movements of Beethoven's Pastoral Symphony to reach. Finally he was seated across from Nicole. For the first time in their relationship, they didn't hug each other *hello*. He wondered for a moment if there was a hidden camera somewhere in the room recording the scene, because the awkwardness between him and the off-putting, but beautiful, woman opposite him, felt too foreign to be reality. And why did she have to wear that black cashmere V-neck sweater that exposed her clavicle and draped her breasts oh, so, perfectly? Wasn't she mad at him? And why was she so dissatisfied with the size of her breasts? A girl with bigger boobs would never be able to rock the impact of that sweater the subtle way it was talking to him right now. Women.

"Hi," he said, and took a sip of water.

Nicole watched Garrett's slender fingers wrap around the crystal vessel, three and a half cubes of ice floating in the clear liquid, condensation dripping down the outside. She knew exactly what came next. After he put down the glass, he would reach for his napkin to dry the moisture off his hand. He never rubbed his hands off on his pants like a lot of guys his age. He was a class act. If they were going to break up, she was really going to miss that.

"Hi," Nicole replied.

"Weird choice for a meeting place."

"Why?"

"You hate this place," he said.

"I wouldn't say I hated it," she replied.

"You hate it."

Nicole rolled her eyes. "We won't be here that long."

"Nice of you to fit me in."

"Excuse me?"

"I thought you'd do more than squeeze me into your busy schedule, that's all. But if that's how important we are to you, so be it."

Nicole's jaw dropped. "How important we are to *me*?"

Garrett knew the instant they were out of his mouth how bad his choice of words had been. Nicole's posture abruptly shifted from her spine's relaxed position against the back of her chair, to sharply leaning towards him.

"I immediately got on a plane to come see you because I wanted you to hear about the Emmy nomination from me, no one else. *That's* how important we are to *me*. And boy, what a stupid idiot I was for ever doing it."

Nicole took a sip of water. She could feel an annoying lump of emotion rising in her throat and she needed something to keep it down. Seeing Garrett again made her realize not only how much she missed him, but how much he'd hurt her, and the wound he'd inflicted may as well have had its own chair at the table. *Don't cry*, she told herself. *Don't you dare cry. Not here. Not in public. Jill will kill you.* Having your emotions always at the surface was an asset in acting class, but in real life it sucked.

The sip she took was the size of two, forcing itself down her esophagus along with an uninvited ice cube. There was nothing worse than a brain freeze on top of trying not to cry.

"I'm sorry about what happened," Garrett blurted out. Nicole waited for whatever he was going to say next, but nothing followed.

"That's it?" she asked. "That's all you have to say?"

Garrett wished he had one of those escape hatches his father showed him the first time he took little Garrett on a tour inside of an aircraft. He was about three years old. It was exciting. This was excruciating.

"You're not even going to tell me who she is?" Nicole interrogated.

He took another sip of water. "She's just a girl I met in a coffee shop."

"In Toronto?"

"No."

"Where, here?"

"Yeah."

"When?"

"A couple months ago."

"Oh, wow. Really? You've been seeing her for a couple months?"

"No, it's not like I've been seeing her. She worked at Lucy's. We struck up a conversation—"

"From what I saw, the two of you were way past conversation—"

"We struck up some conversation. I had an extra ticket to the symphony one night and asked her if she wanted to go. She said, sure. So we did."

"When was that?"

"I don't remember exactly."

"I thought the only couple times you went to the symphony was with me."

"It was that time you couldn't go because of something you had to do for Jill. Some press conference—press junket—at the last minute."

"So this is my fault?"

"I didn't say that."

The waiter approached. "Hi there, I'm Jerome. I'll be your waiter today. Can I tell you about our lunch specials?"

"No," Nicole barked.

"Sorry. Would you like a little more time?" replied Jerome, stymied.

"Yah," interjected Garrett.

Jerome did a 360 and evaporated.

"So all this was going on behind my back?" asked Nicole.

"There was nothing going on. We went to the symphony. That was it."

"Did you have a good time?"

Garrett sighed. "Yeah. We had a good time."

"Tremendous." Nicole took another sip of water.

"That was it."

"Okay, well, that couldn't have been it, Garrett, because unless she teleported herself to Toronto, or teletransmitted—whatever it is people do in your stupid science fiction stories—herself from out of the sky into some random apartment, then she somehow managed to be at your apartment the same time you were. Using the shower… at the same time you were. Which was the same time I happened to walk in, if you can even remember much about that night. I know you were kind of distracted."

Garrett knew this conversation wasn't going to be easy, so he just bore down and plowed through. Telling the whole story was most likely the best way to go here. If there were a flight malfunction, the TSB would demand to know exactly what happened, and require a detailed report be provided before the aircraft was taken up again. This was imperative in order to regain the public's trust and to ensure the safety of everyone concerned, the latter being more important than the former. A little humor would add some much needed brevity at the moment, but Garrett knew any attempt at a joke right now would only offend Nicole. He had hurt her deeply. He just hoped it wasn't irreparable.

"She moved back home. She told me to ring her up next time I was in town."

"She's from Toronto?"

"Mississauga."

"So you knew her from before?"

"No…"

"What's her name?"

Garrett looked around for a jury box filled with twelve stern looking individuals on one side of the room and Darth Vader in a black robe perched high behind a judge's bench on the other, completing the scene he still believed was being filmed.

"Paula. She's no one."

"Mm. I'm sure she'd be thrilled to know you just called her *no one*," Nicole replied with a raised eyebrow that morphed into a roll of both eyes.

Garrett could feel the vibration of the table cloth as it quivered against Nicole's foot. She had a nervous habit of wiggling her foot back and forth whenever she was agitated or upset. The vibration slowed down and Nicole sat back in her chair. Her face was expressionless, her eyes distant.

"It was stupid, Nicky. I shouldn't have rung her up. I was bummed out about Nonie, I guess. I guess I just wanted someone to chat with."

Jerome returned. "Are you ready to order, or would you like more time?"

Nicole didn't look up. The waiter looked at Garrett.

"Um, we don't want anything," Garrett said.

"Nothing?" Jerome inquired with wide eyes.

"I don't think so, sorry," Garrett replied. Jerome whisked their menus off the table and disappeared in a stifled huff.

"Guess I barged in after the chatting segment was over," Nicole said with a somberness Garrett was certain he'd never heard in her before. "My timing's never been great."

They both sat motionless.

Fix this, Garrett's brain instructed. But he didn't know how. Would she forgive him? *Fat chance*, he thought. But it was worth a try. He took a deep breath.

"Can you forgive me?"

Nicole hated that question. It wasn't because she didn't believe there was most likely something really grand about forgiveness (and something, she would learn later in life, that was an essential part of healing). It was because it simply wasn't her strong point. Speaking from her heart, however, was. So she did.

"I don't know. Even if I could, I'm not sure what it is I'd be forgiving."

"What do you mean?"

"I mean, I don't know what to think, Garrett. Do you have feelings for her?"

"She's a nice person, I guess."

"You obviously slept with her—unless you hadn't gotten to that part yet—I mean, I'm sure you didn't end up in the shower 'cause you were just curious how she'd look soaking wet."

"It's not going to happen again," he uttered.

"But how do I know that? There are tons of pretty girls in New York. What if you get lonely again and need someone to talk to? Wait—I was in D.C. for that junket, and I didn't come back till the next day—did you spend the night with her that night?" She saw the answer on Garrett's face. Nicole's shoulders took on another four hundred pounds of the world's weight. "Oh my God. You did. You cheated with her before."

"It's not going to happen again, Nicole."

"It already happened 'again!' You know what, I can't do this."

"Do what?"

"Do you have any idea how hard it is to keep my head on straight in this business? This town can eat you alive and on some days, that's exactly what it feels like. Like you're being eaten alive."

"What does that have to do with anything?"

"It has to do with I don't know if I can handle all that, plus my oh-so-charming, spread-love-and-cheer-to-everyone boyfriend who just can't resist making nice girls laugh."

She shoved her chair back and grabbed her purse.

"Nicky, wait."

"I want you to move out."

Garrett chewed on the words. They didn't taste good. Then from some far off place he heard something he'd overheard Nonie say once to a female friend of hers: *Never stay in a relationship with someone who doesn't want you as much as you want them.*

"Okay," he said.

Nicole wanted it *not* to be okay with him. She wanted him to say something different. But this wasn't a soap opera script.

"Fine! 'Cause I trusted you and I thought we had something that couldn't ever be broken and you ruined it. You treated it like it was something that was just ordinary, and I'm never going to understand why, Garrett. I don't understand why!" The tears finally came. "But it's okay, 'cause I don't need you!"

Nicole wiped her eyes on the back of her palm and marched out of the restaurant. Garrett wanted to run after her and hold her like he always did when she cried. Now he wasn't sure when he'd have the opportunity again, or when the powerful sting delivered by her last words would subside.

Chapter Seventeen

I Burn For You
Sting, 1985

My eyelids opened slowly. I'd been dreaming, and the dream had left me charged with emotion. I struggled to recall it, but couldn't. Then, after a moment, hundreds of people on a narrow street was the picture that drifted into my head, Liam somewhere among them. I could feel the energy of the crowd—alive, exhilarated—though it was far away from me. Liam disappeared farther into the sea of individuals, the back of his head barely visible, but I never lost sight of him. He looked back in my direction, his lips in a soft, tender smile, content in knowing that although he couldn't see me, I would always be able to find him.

I squinted to read the digits on the alarm clock. 2:33 AM. Waking up in the middle of the night meant a lost cause trying to stay awake throughout the day tomorrow. I grimaced, just thinking about the tug of war with exhaustion that lay ahead of me. But my anguish slowly faded as a peaceful, nurturing wave of love enveloped me.

Something warm and comforting was lulling me back to sleep. Something like a mother's arms snuggling her infant to her breast. I slept like a baby in the very same position until the alarm clock woke me five hours later.

Just like every morning, I pressed the snooze button twice before finally turning off the alarm. In the next moment, I reached for the phone. There would be a slew of junk emails, a few that actually required my attention, and Liam's daily *Good morning, love*, which had become the beautiful start to each day. But this particular message from him arrived in the middle of the night.

Getting an early start and wishing I were there to hold you.

The time next to the message was 2:33 a.m., which was 5:33 a.m. Liam's time. I bolted straight up in bed. "No way," I said out loud.

I rubbed my eyes and read the message again. With no ring, no ping, no sound, no vibration against the top of the nightstand even—I always turned the phone off when I went to bed—I woke up in the middle of the night at the very instant Liam had texted me. The Miranda before Liam would have tossed the occurrence off as a coincidence. The Miranda before Liam would've found it just pretty cool and interesting. But this morning, I understood deep in my soul what had taken place. There was no confusion, no mystery. There was only… Liam.

Emotion was reeling inside me. It was all too much, the dream where I saw him in the crowd, the feeling that I'd never lose him, that I'd never leave him, that if he looked back, I'd always be there, the fact that I woke up the moment he reached out to me. Or did I have the dream *because* he reached out to me? It didn't matter.

What mattered was that it was more proof of our undeniable bond. And it was getting stronger. I had to tell him.

MIRANDA: There's something you need to know.

LIAM: I'm all ears.

MIRANDA: Please know it comes from the heart.

I didn't really know how to speak any other way,
whether I was talking to my friends, my children, or even
to a stranger. Good, bad, wrong or right, whatever came
out of my mouth had an industrial strength cord attached
to my heart. And the result could be tremendous or dis-
astrous, depending on the situation.

MIRANDA: It's difficult for me to say.

LIAM: Take all the time you need.

MIRANDA: Okay. Here goes… I'm not sure what this
thing is we're having, but I can't go
backwards from it now.

LIAM: I love you, Miranda. I always have
and I always will.

MIRANDA: I'm not sure I like "always will." Sounds
so final. Like we're never going to see
each other again.

LIAM: Okay. I won't say I always will.

MIRANDA: Here's what you need to know. The truth
of the matter is, I will always be one of
two places in relation to you: standing
still, or moving towards you. But I will
never retreat. Because I'm not able to
retreat now. Do you understand?

LIAM: I do.

MIRANDA: I'm not sure how to explain it. It's just
a feeling I have deep in my soul that I
know to be true like I know my own breath.
You'll just have to trust me.

LIAM: I'm not sure I follow.

MIRANDA: Well, it came to me in a dream last night,
this feeling.

LIAM: What was your dream?

MIRANDA: I had a dream that we got separated
somehow. We were in a crowd.
I mean, I saw you in a crowd. I was
far away from you but I could still see
you, but I don't think you could see me.
But you knew I was there because you
looked back and smiled.

LIAM: Where were we?

MIRANDA: Not sure.

LIAM: That was it?

MIRANDA: Well, not exactly. It's more about
the feeling that came over me when I
woke up from the dream. There was like this
peacefulness that just lulled me back to
sleep. I've never felt a peace like that before.
And it felt like the dream was some kind of
a message. Like no matter what happens,
we would never be separated.

LIAM: And we never will be.

MIRANDA: Do you believe that?

LIAM: Of course.

MIRANDA: Because I will never leave you.
I'll always be here for you, Liam. Oh,
gosh, I'm starting to cry. I'm sorry.

LIAM: Why are you apologizing?

MIRANDA: I don't know.

LIAM: I think that's a beautiful dream.

MIRANDA: There's something else.

LIAM: Okay.

MIRANDA: When I woke up in the middle of the
night, the clock said 2:33. When I got
up this morning, I saw the message you
sent me. It said 2:33, which was 5:33 your
time. That means I woke up in the middle
of the night at exactly the same time you
texted me. And before you say I probably
just heard the phone, my phone was off.

LIAM: I hate when my super powers have a
mind of their own. I didn't even have
my cape on, yet.

MIRANDA: This isn't funny to me.

LIAM: Sorry. I don't mean to be insensitive.
I just hate to think you're crying over this.

MIRANDA: I'm crying because it's just emotional
for me. What's happening here?

LIAM: Do you understand the nature of
connectedness?

MIRANDA: I think so.

LIAM: It's intentional.

MIRANDA: You mean like when I'm sad
you can sense it?

LIAM: Something like that. When I want to
connect with you, I do. I just focus.

MIRANDA: So you really do have super powers.

LIAM: Of course not. Well, not exactly.

MIRANDA: Not exactly?

LIAM: You have it too. If you want.

MIRANDA: Well now you have the ability to wake
me, Liam Kincaid. What's next?

LIAM: Not sure. I've been told people spot me
in cities all over the world although I died
three years ago.

MIRANDA: Uggghh! Didn't I say I wasn't joking?

LIAM: You set it up! How can I resist when
you're always setting me up?

MIRANDA: That was pretty funny, though. I have
to admit it made me laugh.

LIAM: I'm glad, love. Making you laugh is
one of my life's goals.

The laughter Liam brought back into my life was the kind I hadn't experienced in a long time. The kind that forced your whole body and soul to participate. Was it the responsibilities of adulthood that caused me to laugh less over the years? Even Neil said I resisted laughing when he would try to get one out of me. Was it my fault he'd stopped trying? Was my laughter back because I was changing? And was Liam the reason?

Chapter Eighteen

She's Gone
Hall and Oates, 1976

An act of God could not have jostled Gin from Garrett's lap now that she'd found the perfect spot. Her owner sat motionless in the dark, the bright beams of fluorescent shapes shooting out of the television screen providing the only light in the loft. The bowl of stale popcorn was almost empty and there were two warm sips of beer left at the bottom of the can. Garrett pointed the remote at the VCR and rewound the tape for the seventh time. He wanted to see the close up again of Nicole's face when her category was announced.

The camera didn't do her justice. The same was true for her appearances on the soap, not that he ever tuned in regularly. In fact, he stopped watching altogether after they broke up. This one screw up with another girl had certainly placed his life in a weird direction. He couldn't even remember how they ended up in the shower that night. Unbelievable, he thought. All he wanted was one more whiff of whatever that scent was in Paula's hair, and the next thing he knew, he was calling her. Now he understood why women said, "men think with their dicks."

Whenever he thought about that fragrance, somehow his dick got involved.

Then, there was that cute little impish giggle Paula had whenever he told her a dumb joke. He had to admit there was a sweetness about her that he found kind of sexy, not in the same way as Nicole. Nicole was beautiful and captivating and passionate and unpredictable and weakened him in his knees the way they were weakening right now just thinking about her. Nicole was rarely sweet, but when she was, she wasn't even aware of it and that was the kind of sweetness that melted him the most. Nicole had grown from a kid into a woman right alongside him and he refused to accept that they were finished just because she found him with some girl who never should have been there in the first place. Damn, the smell of Paula's shampoo!

He rewound the tape a little farther to the red carpet segment where the celebrities exited their limos and donned the façade of being at ease or else run the risk of their nerves becoming visible to the millions watching on television. Were they really in this much need of the spotlight? Or would half of them be just as content to receive a nice letter in the mail informing them whether they'd won? Would they rather be home in their PJs right now, curled up with a cat and a bowl of popcorn? Garrett had endured these shows because Nicole always insisted he watch them with her, but there were two things he witnessed during the nearly three-hour-long ordeals that he always found interesting: the power that a multitude of designer gowns could have on a female's attention, and how deeply moved Nicole was by the acceptance speeches from the winners who expressed genuine gratitude for the opportunity to simply do what they loved.

"That's really all it's about," Nicole would explain, teary-eyed. "The rest is just a big, dress-up party."

The A-listers were given most of the air time, and Nicole was a newcomer, but one camera managed to steal a substantial shot of her as she stepped out of her shiny black carriage of four wheels, revealing a delicate ankle attached to a black velvet, open-toed stiletto. Caressing the ankle was the hem of a taffeta gown of deep purple. The glistening fabric enclosed her calves in a mermaid's fishtail, and tightly hugged every curve of the rest of her svelte body all the way up through the bodice, stopping just below her delicate shoulders. Around her neck was a huge, pear-shaped pendant Garrett found to be somewhat gaudy, and she was wearing too much make up for his taste, but her raven hair was beautifully swept up, exposing her neck. How he loved that neck. In short, she was stunning. There was simply no getting over, under, or around it. *Stunning with a capital S*, he thought. Nicole waved graciously to the crowd, *Don't Look Back* fans returning their adoration the loudest.

He had gotten used to sharing Nicole with the public, but sharing her with the tux on her arm was another matter. Who the hell was this jerk? He didn't look like anyone from the cast. Some guy from her old acting class who'd rather bleed internally than miss an opportunity to go to the Daytime Emmys, no doubt. And he wasn't even good looking! What pathetic story had this dufus fed her that tugged on her heart strings enough to earn him the title of *Nicole Martin's Escort for the Evening*? And of course, she'd believed it! But the real question was: How could she take anyone other than Garrett? Garrett was the one that truly understood how much this night meant to her. He was the one who watched the glow on her face and the light in her eyes when it was just a dream she talked about at sixteen. Now less than ten years later, the dream had catapulted her exactly on course.

"Can you imagine just being nominated?" she'd say when they were in high school. He couldn't, of course, because it wasn't a thing he longed for, but he remembered how good it felt to bathe in the delight of her musings. And he knew he would be the very first person she'd tell if—oh, geez. *Yep, you fucked up*, a voice confirmed. When the awards were only a week away and he still hadn't heard from Nicole, it was clear she wasn't going to invite him. The half dozen boxes sitting in the middle of the floor of the loft were testimony to that. They were his belongings from the brownstone, still unpacked.

"Fine, if that's the way you want it," he'd told her, and left without argument.

Tonight, only Gin knew how much pain Garrett was in.

"If you could talk, you'd probably have something smart-ass to say, wouldn't you?" he asked the kitty. "Well, before you judge me, let me remind you, you may have belonged to her first, but I adopted you. You have me to thank for not being on the street. You owe me. So why don't you cough up some of her secrets, eh? What do you say?"

Gin meowed.

"What, you didn't like the phrase 'cough up?' Sorry, I thought that was pretty clever… Oh, you want to have a staring contest. Okay. Whoever blinks first has to tell the other a secret about Nicole. But it can't be something dumb, like she watched every single episode of H.R. Puffenstuff when she was a kid. It has to unlock some eternal mystery."

Garrett lifted Gin and cradled the feline snuggly under his chin. Gin purred rhythmically as a teardrop traveled down Garrett's cheek and ended its journey in the soft fur on top of Gin's head.

"It has to help me get her back."

Chapter Nineteen

Beautiful
Christina Aguilera, 2002

Dear Nicky,

Thank you again for the lovely time that you showed me and your daddy. It was so thrilling to be in New York City with you and you were quite the hostess, as usual! Just because you're our daughter doesn't mean we don't appreciate the time you took away from your busy schedule to show us such a good time! It's hard to decide what our favorite tourist spot was. The hotel was beautiful, though you shouldn't have spent that much money on us. We would have been happy with far more modest accommodations. Everyone in Wishton wants to hear about how the Daytime Emmys were! We have been talking about it non-stop, especially the glamorous fashions! As I told you, you looked gorgeous and I think you were right in going with the plum instead of the green. It was stunning on you.

Try not to dwell on the loss, and remember that winning isn't everything. Your father and I are so very proud of you and always have been, from the time you were a little thing. Very few people in your field have accomplished what you have at such a young age. You have your whole life ahead of you and so much more you'll achieve in your career. As you know, mothers are very intuitive, and I wonder if not having Garrett there was a greater disappointment to you than not winning the Emmy. Although it was very nice of your friend Terry to escort you, it was clear that you weren't the same without Garrett there. Hopefully things will work out between the two of you. You and he have been so close for so long. Remember that people make mistakes, and the ones we love are often the ones who hurt us the most. Don't shut him out completely, Nicky. He truly loves you.

Talk to you soon.
Love, Mother

***

"What do you mean they're not renewing my contract?" Nicole asked Jill.

There'd been no easy way to break the news to Nicole. One of the most important functions of the entertainment business was to produce individuals who were experts at sugarcoating the truth with a palpable lie whenever necessary. But Jill's eighteen years in the business taught her that the tougher the message, the tougher the artist. And the sooner a talented kid like Nicole developed the toughness gene, the more successful she would be.

"That's what they said," Jill responded, looking at Nicole with fierce emerald eyes beneath dark auburn bangs that were the natural hair color she was born with. Although Jill's petite stature had earned her a comfortable living as an actress who could always play younger, had she been blessed with a few more inches in height, her career might have brought leading roles that called for fiery, femme fatales—a profile more true to her nature.

Nicole steeled her jaw. "Why not?"

"They don't always give an explanation."

"Don't you think I deserve one?"

"Of course you deserve one."

"Then why didn't you demand one?"

Nicole still had a lot to learn, but her talent for being a brat required no additional training. Jill could feel her own internal pressure cooker starting to boil. "I did! And the answer was, they're simply exploring their options, and meanwhile you'll stay on as a recurring."

"And I'm supposed to be happy with that?"

"No one expects you to be happy about it, Nicole. Anyone who goes into this business to be happy is setting themselves up for disappointment. Happiness is what you get when you're in front of the camera or on the stage doing what you do. When you're outside of that, what you are is a commodity and nothing more. You've heard the stories about entire casts reporting to a set to find out their show was being cancelled?"

"Spare me the details."

"Fine, I'll spare you the details. But I was one of those cast members once. And all we could do after we were done throwing up for several hours, was wipe our tears and start looking for work."

"I'd rather just quit," Nicole said.

"That's crazy!" Jill pounced. "You've carved out the beginning of a great career for yourself, Nicole. There's no reason to shoot yourself in the foot."

"How is it shooting myself in the foot if Larry Ericsson is doing it for me? Is this because I didn't get the Emmy?"

"I don't think so."

"What if it is? Would they do that? I was one of five people in *all* of daytime, up for Best Newcomer, and they don't want to renew my contract because I lost?"

"I really don't think that's it. And if it is, it's not the kind of thing they're ever going to admit."

"So, if I'm so ordinary, tell 'em I quit," Nicole pouted.

"I honestly think that would be a huge mistake."

"Why? You want me to stick around until my character eats a box of poison chocolates or something? What's the point?"

Jill's next words had the tough love of a parent, the protection of a big sister and a dose of don't-shoot-the-messenger.

"There was one other thing they said that I think might be beneficial for you to know…"

Nicole crossed her arms over her chest in defiance. She couldn't believe there was more.

"They think your work has gotten, well, a little mediocre."

"What? Is that what they said?"

Jill nodded *yes*.

"I am *not* mediocre!"

"No, you're not. And they know you can do better and they've seen a decline, that's all."

Nicole was silent. It was like walking in on Garrett and Sudsy Visitor all over again. First, the shell-shock, then the pain.

"I lost my boyfriend. I lost my show. What's next? I really would just rather leave the show, Jill."

"Why? It'll just make you look bad."

"Why would it make me look bad if they're not renewing anyway?"

"Then at least don't leave until you have something else."

"I'm not worried about finding something else. Maybe 'Love Me Forever' has something. Can't we set up a meeting with Randy? I don't know, maybe I'll just go home and see my folks. Take a break."

"Do you ever talk to Garrett?"

"No! And why does everyone keep asking about him? Is that supposed to help me?" Nicole attacked. "Why does anyone give a shit? I certainly don't."

"Cuz, honey, you seem kind of depressed. You haven't been the same since you guys broke up, and it shows." It was the one and only time in the conversation Jill took the liberty of sugarcoating. The actual truth was that Nicole's split with Garrett was not only ruining her work, it was taking meat off her bones, the light from her eyes, and the energy from her spirit. "People are just concerned about you, that's all."

"Well, you can tell people, including yourself, to stop it, I'm fine."

Jill gave Nicole an *I don't believe you* look.

"Really, I am. And, besides, there's plenty of fish in the sea… Anyway, tell Larry I quit."

Jill watched, disappointed, as her favorite client took her heavy load of one part talent and one part attitude, placed it onto her young shoulders, and marched out of the office.

Chapter Twenty

All I Do
Stevie Wonder, 1980

Liam's face was just inches from mine. None of my dreams had even come close to the thrill of this moment and I was certain my heart beat could be heard outside my body. No matter how a person may change physically over the years, the eyes never do. I looked into his eyes; glanced at his mouth. His mouth, his mouth… *Oh, God.* He brought his lips to mine and everything that existed outside of us disappeared. His arms encircled my back and he pulled me close, embracing me tighter until I couldn't move. I slipped one arm around him while my other hand slid behind his head and clasped the silky waves of his hair. The softness of his lips belied the cold climate where he made his home. He smelled of vanilla shaving balm and crisp lake air and I opened my mouth wider as his lips caressed mine with the same hunger he had for chocolate and brandy and life. We were both breathing heavier now and I grew dizzy. When his tongue went into my mouth, it sent a surge through my pelvis that raced through my entire body. Then I heard a car horn honking.

The light had turned green.

***

Fortunately, no one was home to detect how shook up I was over this little episode on the road. I slammed the door to the garage behind me and threw my keys on the coffee table. *That's what comes from being over tired,* I told myself, although I couldn't deny that in this case it was plain, old-fashioned, daydreaming, that could've proved treacherous for me, or someone else, behind the wheel. All I wanted was One Normal Thought about Liam. Was that too much to ask? Detached, fleeting, occasional. That's how I wanted to think of him. Yes, that was the word— *occasional*—instead of *perpetual*, which seemed to be the progressive state of things. But who was I kidding? Fighting to concentrate on anything other than Liam had become a daily chore.

Cut yourself some slack. It's your writing you're passionate about, not Liam. Without passion, you can't put words on the page. There are characters and plots and schemes and themes you're responsible for. It's your job to fantasize.

I decided I'd keep repeating this to myself until My Self was convinced.

I stopped at the mirror in the foyer to remove the beginning of a tiny cobweb I discovered in the corner of its frame. Over four feet high, oblong shaped and encased in hand-carved mahogany set inside thick, wrought iron rods, the weight of this mirror had required both the store

133

owner, quite a burly guy himself, and one of his workers to put it in my car. I'd hoped Neil would like it. But I'd hoped he'd understand my inexplicable attachment to its beauty, more.

I made eye contact with the woman looking back at me.

Are you writing the book, missy, or is the book writing you?

MIRANDA: The character of Garrett is starting to get interesting.

LIAM: In your book?

MIRANDA: Yeah. His sense of humor is his greatest quality, of course, because he's a younger
version of you.

LIAM: Oh, c'mon, no one's as funny as me.
Not even me.

MIRANDA: LOL—silly boy. But what I need to reveal is
how it's a safety mechanism for him.

LIAM: I hope you've made him incredibly good looking.

MIRANDA: I need to show that he's not just quick-witted, but that he wears his sense
of humor like a protective armor.

LIAM: Do I get a matching helmet?

MIRANDA: See, like that. You just did it.

LIAM: Did what?

MIRANDA: You know what.

LIAM; Inserted humor in order to avoid the topic of who I am deep inside?

MIRANDA: Yes.

LIAM: Can't argue with you there.

MIRANDA: And I want to chisel away at all your layers to get to the man underneath.

LIAM: Chisel away.

Chapter Twenty-One

Wishing On a Star
Rose Royce, 1978

Satisfied with the explanation that sleep deprivation was responsible for the ills of my afternoon, I decided a nap was in order. A nap was the cure for so many things. A nap was on that list of items children hate when they're little but grow to love when they're adults, like onions or shrimp or a day with nothing to do.

The tiny lump of plaster on the ceiling above the bed was most likely more distinct before the acoustic was scraped off. I wondered if it had to fight to maintain its spot among the other tiny lumps of plaster. Was it proud to resemble what looked like the shape of Minnesota? Or was it Illinois? Geography had always been one of my favorite subjects but I was never any good at identifying the U.S. states by their shapes.

I fixed my eyes on the speck of plaster while Gianni Vancini's *All of My Life* floated through my ear buds. It was better this way, to lie motionless and form a relationship with the spot on the ceiling while waiting for the sound of the saxophone to drown out everything else. It might have even qualified as meditation if I could manage to quiet my thoughts and hold my body completely still. But all I wanted was to go to sleep, if only for thirty minutes, and there were so many thoughts keeping me awake.

I had to try harder. I pulled an age-old relaxation exercise out of my hat that I'd learned in one of my drama classes at college. I closed my eyes and with the isolation of each muscle, tried to set my mind free. But the thoughts remained like items on a check-list:

That I couldn't remember the last time Neil kissed me.

How the walls of the bedroom were still white instead of the warm, gentle taupe I'd planned to paint them ten years ago.

That I hadn't been back to book club in two months.

If Neil knew another man had stolen my heart, would he even care?

That I was still working as a proofreader for the same 'list of colleges and universities' website for college bound students that I thought five years ago was going to be a temporary job.

What children think of you when they discover their parents are just real people trying to do the best they can with real life.

Was Liam having a good time on his vacation?

In a few minutes, I'd grown significantly drowsy. If this had been a real assignment in a real class, I believe I would have gotten an 'A.'

I imagined sitting across from Ms. Hamilton at Carnegie.

"So, how do you think you did?" Hamilton asked me in her delicate way.

"I think I did okay."

"You did better than okay. You did very well, in fact. The point was not to move a muscle and take inventory of what that felt like. What did you get from it?"

"Greece."

"Greece?" Her eyes wide as she elongated the word.

"Yes. Greece is finally here. I've been knowing about it for weeks. Well, that it was coming. I did okay, at first. But knowing he's so far away just makes me long for him more."

"Him, meaning Liam?"

I leaned in to her, grinning like a best friend with a secret that we both knew she already knew, unsure why she was playing dumb. "Um... of course... who else would we be talking about?"

"But you're still talking to him. I'm unclear how his being in Greece changes anything. How does it—change anything?"

"I don't know."

"He's there with—"

"His wife."

"Does that bother you?"

"No. That's as it should be."

"Are you sure?"

"Of course." But I wasn't being entirely truthful. And I felt I needed to be. If not to Hamilton, at least to myself. I elaborated. "I mean, well, maybe I'm just a little scared things will be different when he comes back."

"In what way?"

That he'll pack up his music and leave, I thought. *That his relationship with me was all just fun and games for him. That he'll gain a sudden sense of conscience that reminds him he's married and won't talk to me anymore. Hell, pick one.* I made an effort to zero in on what it really was that I feared might change. "That he'll come back loving me less." It hurt to say it.

"But he said he'd always love you, didn't he?" Hamilton asked gently.

"Yeah."

"And you used the word 'scared.' What is it about this situation that's causing you to feel afraid?"

"That while they're over there, maybe he'll remember why he married her in the first place. Isn't that what exotic vacations with your spouse are supposed to do?"

"Sometimes," Hamilton mused. "But breathtaking environments are rarely the best things by which to measure the depth of our feelings for someone."

"Anyway, it doesn't matter."

"Of course, it matters, Miranda."

"Why?"

"Because your feelings matter. Why wouldn't they?"

"My feelings are irrelevant."

"You know that isn't true."

"My feelings about Liam are—"

"Complex, I know."

"Complex or not, they're irrelevant in the scheme of things."

"Because?"

"Because… That isn't it, really."

"Then, what do you believe it is?"

It felt stupid to admit that—*it*—was an overwhelming sense of entitlement I felt where everything having to do with Liam was concerned. I'd earned a special place in his heart and he'd earned a special place in mine. But I wasn't going to get Hamilton to understand the depth of my love for Liam any more than I could understand it myself. I tried to simplify it. "He's never been to Greece before. It's a new experience for him. I want to share every new experience with him, and I can't."

"I see."

"It should be me."

"I'm sorry."

"I should be the one who's there with him."

"Because you're in love with him?"

"It should be me because the stars are up there, shining every night, shining and laughing, laughing and shining, like they're sharing some great big joke at my expense. Like they know they made some huge mistake."

"As though, by some means, an alignment occurred that was improper?" Hamilton probed in her angelic tone.

"I know it sounds stupid."

"No, no, not stupid, at all. I'm simply trying to establish clarity."

I thought of the perfect example that would clarify it for Hamilton.

"Liam and I were, how can I say, a 'connection interrupted,' like Catherine and Heathcliff."

"Ahh. *Wuthering Heights*, a great literary classic."

"Yes! Isn't it an amazingly beautiful story? You see, it didn't matter that Cathy and Heathcliff went off and married other people and had kids with other people and all the things that happened in between. They were eternally connected."

"'Eternally.' Such a beautiful word. A strong word."

I frowned. "You don't think that's possible between two people?"

"Oh, I do. But you think it's possible, and that's all that matters," she reassured me.

"I do."

"Ms. Brontë's story was a tragic one, though. The relationship was driven by obsession and greed and passion and revenge. Remember what Heathcliff said when she died? 'Catherine Earnshaw, may you not rest while I am living.'"

"'If you say I've killed you, haunt me then… drive me mad…'" I recited.

Hamilton continued, "'… but do not leave me in this abyss where I cannot find you…'"

"'… for I cannot live without my life…'" I mused.

"'… I cannot live without my soul,'" Hamilton sighed, placing her hand on her heart.

Teacher and student shared a smile.

"Anyway, sometimes it's just too much to think about. Liam, I mean. He's too much. He can wake me just by thinking about me, did I tell you that? Not the same way two close friends cross each other's minds at the same time. But actually *wake* me. Pretty cool, huh? It frightened me at first, knowing he can do that. Now I take it for granted. But sometimes it's all just too much. And I thought if I held every single muscle really still, I wouldn't feel anything. Or think anything."

"Well, you did a good job, Miranda," she beamed.

"I'm happy for him, you know?" I beamed back.

"Are you?"

"Yes. I'm happy that he's having a marvelous time. I never thought I'd feel that way about it. Even though I'm scared, I'm really happy for him. That's how much I love him."

"I think that's wonderful, Miranda, to feel that way about another human being. It means Liam can trust you with his heart."

Hamilton evaporated from my imagination and the tones of Vancini's saxophone filled my brain again. Then, whatever it was that the music pushed into the dark void inside me, a well of tears was forced up and out. The water from my eyes came strong and fast, carried by some profound sadness. Was it that Liam was in some beautiful, exotic place while I was stuck here with my suffocating loneliness? Was it that those treasured times—when a positive critique from my drama teacher made me float on air—were gone, and with them, my youth? As the rhythmic strains of the melody grew to a fever pitch, I felt myself slow dancing in Liam's arms. I closed my eyes tighter, hoping that when I opened them, something—anything—about my life, would look different.

Chapter Twenty-Two

Smaointe
Enya, 1991

Scotland was, by far, a place that Garrett had greatly underestimated. Hollywood movies and stories he'd heard when he was a little boy had left him with an uninformed impression of what this first visit to the roots of his ancestry would be like. He expected the city of Edinburgh to be cold, bleak and industrial. It was, instead, a cosmopolitan center of various cultures, with the sound of Russian, German, Chinese, Spanish and English being spoken in the crowded streets. The skin tones were white, black, brown and yellow, and there were as many hijabs as there were yarmulkes.

His father had made time for a tour of Stirling Castle, birthplace of Mary Queen of Scots and home to Robert the Bruce, from where William Wallace 'Braveheart' launched his raids against the invading English. Standing where they stood, walking the pathways they walked, scanning the same horizon they scanned, was an emotional experience for Garrett. Now from the top of

Arthur's Seat, the two gazed out at Edinburgh Castle where it dominated the skyline high up at the end of the Royal Mile. From this high perch, the town was virtually impervious to attack in the time of land wars. It had served as a palace, a garrison, a prison, and was now a historic part of the National Trust. The view extended far across the port of Edinburgh, over the Firth of Forth toward the village of St. Andrews. The lowlands were even more green than Garrett could have ever imagined, and surprisingly lush from regular rains arising from the North Sea and the Atlantic. The highlands were rocky, craggy and dramatic—and so were the people. The heart of Scotland was in the highlands. The people were tough and self-reliant. Now he knew where his father had gotten it from.

With only a half mile to go, father and son approached the end of their hike to Dunsapie Loch. Garrett was surprised how heavy a box of ashes of such a tiny person could be. But he'd volunteered to carry it for a while so his father wouldn't have to. The two looked around for a quiet spot near the edge of the water where they'd be afforded some privacy from the tourists.

"Over there," James motioned.

He was pointing to a vacant park bench a few yards away. He reached over and carefully took the box from Garrett, then slowly removed the container inside. Garrett knew there were most likely words his father had prepared for this moment, but he had no idea what he had in mind. He waited patiently while his father collected his thoughts. When James finally spoke, what he said took Garrett by surprise.

"Do you have anything you'd like to say, son?"

Garrett was stunned. "Me?"

"Well, seeing how it's just the two of us, yes, it was to you that I was referring."

"Um, I didn't really prepare anything."

"Me, either. So, here goes. God, if you're really up there, you need to know there's not a better spirit that you could be taking back under your wing. There was no better wife to her husband, bastard that he was—"

Garrett released a chuckle that he'd intended to stifle, but his dad shot him a forgiving glance.

"—and no better mum to her children. She'll be missed beyond description and if angels are real, she'll be a standout among your employees, of that I'm certain. So, Nona Gwen McKinnon, may you rest peacefully here with the beauty of your heritage surrounding you. I love you, Mom."

James removed the lid of the box and emptied the contents along the edge of the water as a gentle wind lifted the last of the ashes into the air. He took a handkerchief from his pocket and wiped his eyes while Garrett discovered the lump in his own throat.

"Bye, Nonie," he whispered, hoping his grandmother would hear.

For the next few minutes, the two sat quietly. A fierce ray of sun pierced the cloud cover over Arthur's Seat that, for the entire day, had threatened drizzle. The spot where they were sitting became so warm that Garrett had to open the snaps at the neckline of his jacket to get some relief from the sudden heat. A parade of geese performed a dance for their audience of two, and as father and son watched the feathered troupe, they silently embraced the joy of being in the other's company. With each breath the father regained from the son the remnants of a past youth, while the son felt his young soul expand by the experiences of his father. Whatever lines they believed defined their differences, blurred to the point of being invisible, and as the things they allowed to divide them faded away, all that remained was love.

"Do you remember the little suburb I pointed out to you on the way here?" James asked.

"Yeah. 'Bird' something. Where Nonie and Pop lived."

"Burdiehouse."

"Uh-huh."

"Well, there's property there that still belongs to the family. Your grandmother left it to you and your brothers."

"She did?"

"Yup. It's two lots. One's got an abandoned barn house on it, and the other's empty. They're not in the best of condition, but they're yours just the same."

"Wow. What do you want us do with it?"

"Well, that's up to you and your brothers, now. You'll have to talk it over with each other and decide if you want to sell it or rebuild on it or keep it. But in another year the government will take it, so you need to act soon, eh?"

"Sure is beautiful here. Now I know why she loved it."

"Yup, she did. But the land of opportunity was in North America, so she and your grandfather left before I was born."

"Do you think she was sad to leave?"

"Oh, most likely. But not for long."

"Didn't you take vacations here when you were little?"

"No. We didn't come back here until I was in my twenties. That was the first time I'd ever been here. The only thing I knew of Scotland was what I'd seen in photographs. She always said she wanted to come back one more time. Guess that was today, eh?"

Chapter Twenty-Three

Will You Still Love Me
Chicago, 1986

"You're awfully young, son," James said to Garrett as he pulled the car over to the curb in front of the apartment building in Liberty Village.

"But you said it made sense," he told his dad.

"I said it was the right thing to do."

"Well, I'm either too young, or it's the right thing to do. Which is it?"

"It's both," his father replied. "And it will have its pros and cons just like everything else in life."

"Thanks for the ride. Beats the shuttle."

"This was a good trip, Garrett."

"Scattering Nonie all over the Scottish countryside?" Garrett replied.

"Don't be disrespectful. That wasn't what I meant."

"Sorry. Yeah, it was. A good trip, I mean."

"I enjoyed our time together."

"Me, too."

"I could have done without some of your wise remarks but that's to be expected."

"You laughed at every one of them!" Garrett recalled proudly.

"As a matter of fact, I did."

Garrett smiled at his father's admission and hopped out of the car. "You'd better get going. You're wasting fuel. Oh—and your music selection sucks. You need to get out of the Dark Ages and get some new tunes. Do you even have anything other than that Henry Mancini tape?"

"You played my favorite song from that tape everyday on the piano when you were little."

"Because you wouldn't feed me, if I didn't."

"Seemed like a fair trade, to me," James shouted through the window as his foot depressed the gas pedal. The car disappeared down the street.

Though his father didn't always show it, the love he had for his sons was something they always felt, and something Garrett knew would always be there. He wondered if he would be as good a father to his own kids when the time came. He hoped so, anyway.

Garrett walked into the loft and dropped his duffel bag. Before he could turn on the lights, out of nowhere Gin dove for the floor from somewhere above Garrett's head and glued herself to his calf. Garrett picked her up, nuzzling his face to hers.

"One day you're going to make me fall and break my neck, you know that? And it'll be days before anyone finds my body."

Garrett tossed the cat affectionately back to the floor. He grabbed a Budweiser out of the fridge and strolled over to the chest of drawers where a tiny blue velvet box was housed. With the box in one hand and the beer in the other, he collapsed onto the couch.

What if she said *no*? He prayed that wouldn't happen. Then it occurred to him he didn't know the first thing about praying. What if it didn't work because he wasn't doing it correctly? His mom had dragged him to church enough times as a young boy for him to have some sense of how to do it, not that he had ever paid attention. But what reason would she have to say *no*, he thought? He was sure she wanted to get married. They already knew each other well, and they would have their entire lives to get to know each other better.

His mother and father certainly seemed happy all these years. Had his father been this nervous about proposing? They'd just spent nearly a week together and Garrett had forgotten to ask him. He also forgot to mention he'd already bought a ring. What he wasn't sure about, was whether she'd be pissed at him for just showing up on her doorstep with no specific plans, no fancy dinner reservations, no dramatic presentation. But she had to know him well enough by now to know he was a nonconformist and, given the opportunity, he would always go against the grain. He suspected she liked that about him. If she didn't, she was in for a lot of frustration down the road. At the very least, he would get down on one knee. In that regard, he was his father's son. It would just be wrong not to. But if he were going to do it tonight, he needed to make a decision soon. It was not quite 4:30. If he left now and drove fast, he could still get there before dark.

***

Garrett stood outside her front door. His palms were sweaty and he tried to hold the panic at bay.

You're going to just appear out of nowhere after everything that's happened and expect that the mere sight of you will make her instantly melt and wrap her arms around you? he asked himself.

Idiot, was the answer.

Maybe this whole thing really was a mistake. Maybe he would just say he wanted to see her and not take the ring out at all. Or maybe she wouldn't be home. That would take care of everything!

He took a deep breath. He pushed the buzzer then counted the seconds it normally took her to answer. Her voice came through the speaker device.

"Who is it?"

"Hey, Paula. It's Garrett."

Chapter Twenty-Four

Friends
Bette Midler, 1973

"Believe that what's true for you, is true for every-one." Nicole told Kelly.

The junior high school student was one of fifteen others in the summer drama workshop at Wishton Community Center and none of them could believe their teacher was a famous TV actress who had grown up right there in their hometown.

"You're prettier than you are on TV," one of the boys said, followed by a resounding mix of laughter and admonishment by his peers.

"Thank you, I think?" said Nicole, as another round of adolescent giggles filled the room.

"What do you mean true for everyone?" Kelly asked.

"I mean that sometimes an actor will have an instinct about a behavior that feels right, but they'll doubt it, or question it, so they won't try it. They'll second guess themselves and think, *well I might do that, but maybe it's not what my character would do*. When the truth of the matter is, more often than not what feels right to you can be just as valid for someone else—like your character. And if it turns out to not be the right choice, you'll know. But in the beginning, assume what's right for you could be right for everyone."

"Miss Martin, it's after two," one of the students said.

"Oh my goodness, sorry. I gotta let you guys go. Read that scene I gave you from Romeo and Juliet. We're going to talk about it next time. And I told you, call me Nicole!"

The kids filed out of the converted recreation hall. Nicole was not far behind them when she noticed the boy who paid her a compliment was stalling. He was much taller than Nicole would have guessed from the impression of him seated criss-cross style on the floor for close to three hours. His nearly-adult body was topped with the sweet, round face of an inquisitive boy.

"Ms. Martin—I mean, Nicole?"

"Hi," smiled Nicole. "Trey, right?"

"Troy."

"I'm sorry," Nicole blushed.

"Oh, no, it's okay. You've got to remember twenty names, we only have to remember one."

"That's funny, my mother used to say that."

"I know. My sister had your mom a couple years ago," he said.

"Really?" Nicole beamed.

"Yeah. My sister has kind of a complicated name, and your mom was always getting it wrong. So my sister used to come home all the time going, 'You all have just one name to remember. I have thirty.'"

Nicole chuckled. "What was your sister's name?"

"Sharynaskaya."

"Oh, wow! That's a mouthful!"

"I know," Troy chuckled.

"And how did you end up with something simple like Troy?"

"It's really Trotinskayov, but my parents decided to shorten it when I started school."

"Oh my gosh! And your last name's Nazarov. So, your family's Russian, I take it?"

"Yeah."

"I have to lock up. Want to walk out with me?"

"Sure. I just had a quick question," Troy said.

"Shoot."

"We read a little bit of Romeo and Juliet in school last year and I hated it. Can I pick something else?"

"You know, if your first introduction to Shakespeare is not with a teacher who knows how to make it real and exciting and relevant to your life now, you can come away with a terrible feeling about it. I'm hoping when we play with the scenes, they'll seem real to you and you can get excited about the language."

"Well, it's not really that. I mean, Mr. Rosen was pretty good and he helped the language make sense and all. I just don't get how two people that young—like, well, pretty much my age, I guess, cuz, well I'm 15—can love each other so much that they're willing to die for each other."

"Do you have a girlfriend?"

"No."

"Anyone you like?"

"Uhm, sorta," his round cheeks turning a light crimson.

"Does she know it?"

"Uhm, I don't know."

"But you've talked to her."

"Yeah."

"And the first time you talked to her, were you nervous?"

"A lot!"

"And when you weren't talking to her, or when she wasn't around, did you find yourself thinking about the next chance you'd get to talk to her?"

"Yeah."

"Thinking about it a lot?"

"Yeah," Troy replied with embarrassment.

"So, on a scale of 1 to 10, where do you rank this girl—for you?"

"Uhm, like a 12."

Nicole laughed. "Alrighty, then. Here's my point. Romeo's feelings are no different from what you would feel in the same situation. You might not be deeply, crazy in love with this girl, but I can tell by the way you're talking about her and from the look on your face that she *affects* you. That's the point. And it's distracting, right?"

Troy blushed. "Uhm, a little. Sometimes. I mean, it's not like I walk around in a daze or anything."

"But you think about her a lot when she's not around?"

"Yeah."

"Okay. Well, Juliet is a 12 for Romeo, too. Those are the feelings we're going to start with when we do the scene work. It's a perfect play for you guys because both of the characters are around your age. And the feelings you have at your age, for another person, are really powerful. So, give it a chance. I promise when we're done, I'll have you loving Romeo and Juliet."

Troy smiled. "Was it that powerful for you, the first time you fell in love?"

Nicole knew the answer instantly, but hesitated in order to make sure her response would be free of any hidden regret. She looked directly at Troy and smiled.

"Yes. It was."

"Are you still together? I mean, if you don't mind my asking. Cuz, you're still kinda young."

"No, we're not."

"Oh, sorry."

"Don't be sorry. Because, see, I think, because it was so very powerful, and I was really young, I'm not sure I could ever feel that way again. I don't know if it's possible."

"Gotcha," Troy nodded.

"Well, that's good. Because I'm not sure I totally get it, myself. See you next week," Nicole replied.

Troy caught up with his friends, leaving Nicole alone with her melancholia, her loneliness, her memories of Garrett.

***

Instead of driving straight home, she stopped to take a stroll through downtown. It was awkward living with her parents again after being out of the house since she was eighteen. But it was only going to be for a few months, so Nicole tried to focus on all the good things about being back home. The only real negative was trying to avoid conversation about Garrett. It seemed like everyone wanted to talk about him. Who was next? The President himself? Did the White House find her break up with Garrett paramount to everything else going on in the world?

The storefronts along the promenade varied from new and unrecognizable to worn and warmly familiar. It felt good to be among the late afternoon crowd which was just lean enough to allow a relaxing walk without having to maneuver through a ton of shoppers. The awning outside Micelli's shoe store had a different logo than the one Nicole remembered. Mr. Micelli was a sweet, round, affectionate soul who brought a smile to the face of everyone he encountered. His warmth ran in his family and his daughter, Veronica, had been a friend of Nicole's in high school. Nicole stepped into the store and waited patiently to see how long it would take before Mr. Micelli recognized her.

"Good afternoon," he said.

"Good afternoon," Nicole smiled.

Mr. Micelli did a double take, and then squeezed Nicole with his robust, Santa Claus-like arms.

"Oh my goodness!! Little Nicole Martin?"

"Hi!"

"Oh my goodness, so good to see you! Are you back home? I heard you're a big star living in New York now!"

Nicole giggled. "Well, I don't know about big star."

"Yeah, on the TV soap operas they said! Look at you! Still so beautiful just like when you were a little girl!"

"Aww, thank you!"

"So you're in town for a visit?"

"Yeah, for a little while."

"I run into your folks now and then. I bet they're glad to have you home. Veronica's going to be sorry she missed you. She just left a little while ago."

"Oh, no. How's she doing?"

"She's doing great. She's working for me, now, you know."

"That's wonderful! Will you tell her I said 'hi'?"

"Of course, sweetie! How long are you here for?"

"Not sure. Another month, maybe."

"Well, we'll keep watching for you on the TV. We knew you'd go far."

"You're sweet."

A woman entered the shop with a look on her face that telegraphed a specific question.

"Excuse me, one second, Nicole," Micelli said.

"No, it's fine. I just wanted to say 'hi.' Love the new sign, by the way."

"Thanks, sweetie. You take care and give Ronnie a call."

Nicole walked back out onto the promenade. When she glanced over her shoulder for another look at the little shop that held happy memories of hanging out with the owner's daughter after school, she collided with a female shopper coming from the opposite direction.

"Oh, sorry!" Nicole said.

"Sorry!" the girl echoed.

Nicole recognized her instantly.

"*Diane?*"

The young woman spun around and faced Nicole.

"*Nicole?*"

The squeals of delight that followed were enough to wake the quail at Terrace Lake, and the smiles glued across the girls' faces had not changed since they were youngsters.

***

It was cozy inside the walls of the Bobcat, a popular pub tucked in the middle of College Town. Its dark, woodsy interior wrapped itself around the two old friends, fulfilling their teenage fantasies of being able to frequent the establishment as legal age drinkers. The rite of passage felt glorious.

"I always knew you'd pick something noble and worthwhile to go into, something that would make a difference in the world. Wish I had done that," Nicole told Diane.

Diane tossed back the last sip of her second Coors and motioned to the bartender to bring another round. "Why?" she giggled.

Diane had a wonderful laugh that was void of even the slightest ounce of insincerity. "You're a big TV actress making tons of money! You're living your dream. How many people get to do that?"

"It's not rocket science."

"Neither is what I'm doing. I fill software orders for hospital computers. No one's life is getting saved by doing that."

"Ohhhh, you don't know, though," Nicole replied. "Maybe not directly. But it's for hospitals. Hospitals help people when they're sick."

"Yeah, but I don't want to do it my whole life."

"You won't."

"Ohhhh, you don't know, though," mocked Diane with a tipsy grin anchoring itself across her face.

"Yeah, I do."

"No, you don't."

"You know, this is the first time I've been in here," Nicole mused.

"Really?" Diane replied, wide-eyed.

"Really."

"Not even with a fake I.D.?"

"Are you kidding? Mrs. Martin's daughter? Can you imagine if I got caught using a fake I.D.?"

"You never even came in here after college?"

"Nope. I didn't come back here, remember?"

"Oh, that's right. It was just us three nerds, me, John, and Curtis who stayed. You and Garrett got out of here. Good for you… You heard about Curtis, right?"

Nicole felt that flip in her stomach again. "That he's in Mitchelson?"

"Yeah."

"Yeah. Sad."

"I had no idea there was anything wrong with him," Diane said dismally. "Guess sometimes you just don't see stuff. You think someone's fine and you don't realize they're actually ill."

"None of us knew there was anything wrong with him," Nicole replied.

"I know. He seemed normal."

"Normal? I don't know that I'd go that far. Using some alter ego name all the time wasn't exactly 'normal.'"

"Normal for him, I guess," shrugged Diane. "C'mon, you have to admit, we were all a little weird."

"How was I weird?" demanded Nicole.

"Well, you weren't exactly weird. Just dramatic," Diane giggled.

"Oh. Yeah. Well, can't argue with you there."

"Where the hell is our waiter? I thought he was bringing me another beer? And now you're getting paid to be," Diane beamed. "So it's perfect… Didn't Curtis try to go visit you or something?"

"Yep. He tried."

"Really? Ewww."

"That's a story for another night."

Nicole squeezed the tiny pink plastic straw in her piña colada and stirred. She stared into the liquid, trying to find a way to change the subject, but Diane did it for her.

"What's weird is Garrett getting married. All of a sudden I get this wedding invitation in the mail. Talk about being out of the loop."

Nicole felt the oxygen start to seep out of the Bobcat, making it difficult for her to breathe. Every additional word from Diane's mouth sent the floor rising closer towards Nicole's knees. She steadied herself onto the bar stool. Diane's mouth continued to move.

"I wonder how long he and this girl were going out. Do you know her?"

Nicole's gaze shifted from the liquid inside her glass to Diane's face. Diane wondered if her friend had heard a word she'd said, but when she saw Nicole's expression, something between panic and paralysis, she realized Nicole had heard every syllable.

"Oh my God, you didn't know," Diane gasped, bringing both hands to her face, covering her mouth. "Oh my God, I'm sorry. I thought you knew."

A smudge on top of the bar counter in the shape of a slightly deformed fifty-cent piece stole Nicole's attention. Using her cocktail napkin, she began to rub the spot. The phony laughter of a middle aged woman on what appeared to be a miserable date with a disheveled grad student, drifted through the atmosphere from the other side of the room. Nicole glanced up for a second to find the couple, and went back to rubbing the smudge. Removing it entirely was going to require more elbow grease, but it was nothing a little furniture polish couldn't eliminate. Nicole wasn't sure whose voice asked Diane the next question, because it certainly didn't feel like her own.

"Garrett's getting married?"

Diane couldn't remember a time she'd felt this awful about something she'd said.

"Yeah. I'm sorry."

"Don't be sorry," said Nicole.

"I mean, I'm sorry I said anything."

"Why? Better than me reading about it in the Wishton High Alumni news column… When? Is he getting married, I mean?"

"Um, couple months, I think. I thought you were—well, of course, you weren't—it was stupid of me to think you got an invitation. I was thinking maybe you two still talked, or that you were still friends. So I thought you knew."

"I'm happy for him."

Diane's eyes widened to the size of saucers. "You're *happy* for him?"

"I am," Nicole confirmed.

"That's bullshit and you know it. Even if you *had* known about it, it's bullshit. You don't have to be happy for him, Nicole."

"I kind of am, though," Nicole insisted.

"Right. Which is why, 'oh, that's great!' came right out of your mouth when I told you. C'mon. And why would you be, anyway?" Diane said, rolling her eyes.

"Why not? Can't I be happy for him?"

The waiter appeared with Diane's Coors.

"Thanks… Of course, you can. But you looked like you were going to throw up a minute ago. And that's understandable. Everyone knows you two were meant for each other."

"Well, apparently not. Wait—what do you mean, 'everyone knew?' It's not like we ever went out, really. I was going out with Curtis."

"I know, but everyone knew you were in love with Garrett."

"How?"

"It was just obvious, or something, I don't know. There was something intense between the two of you whenever you were in the same room."

"And I thought I hid it, so well," Nicole sighed.

"'Fraid not," Diane told her friend.

"How come you never told me how obvious I was?"

"I don't know. I guess because, well, maybe I figured it was just a crush. It wasn't just you. It was him, too."

"I wanted to be with him so bad."

"Well, you finally got your wish." Diane raised her glass, as in a toast. Then the tone of her voice shifted to serious. "What happened, anyway? Why did you guys break up?"

Nicole took in a long deep breath, and exhaled it slowly. "Let's put it this way. Never, never, ever show up at a guy's apartment unannounced unless you're prepared to get your heart broken. No matter if you have a key. No matter how committed the two of you are. No matter how cool you think it would be to surprise him. Don't do it. Always call ahead."

Diane, about to swallow a mouthful of brew, put down her beer and dropped her jaw, as though her chin were attached to the rim of her glass by an invisible string, forcing her mouth open. "No!"

"Yep."

"You caught him with somebody?"

"Yep."

"Oh my God, what a pig!"

"Yep."

"In your apartment?"

"Nope. Well, not the New York apartment, *his* apartment—the one he keeps in Toronto. Keeps, kept… I wanted to tell him in person about my Emmy nomination so I flew there to surprise him."

"That's horrible, Nicole. You must've been devastated."

"Pretty much."

"Were they… doing it?"

"No, not when I walked in. When I walked in they were taking a shower together. I'm not sure if they had just finished doing it or if they were about to do it. I didn't stick around to see how things would progress."

Diane seemed suddenly sad. "Geez… I can't believe it. I mean, Garrett? I know he's just a guy, but I still can't believe it."

"You hear about that happening to people, but it's so weird when it happens to you. It's surreal."

"Is this the same girl?"

"Is who the same girl?"

"The one he's marrying. Is she the same one he was with when you walked in on them?"

"Oh, I don't know. I'm over him, anyway."

"Yeah, sure," Diane quipped.

"Let him go get married, if that's what makes him happy."

"He doesn't deserve to be happy. He deserves a big punch in the nose! Right between the eyes!" Diane started to laugh. "So he falls flat on his ass! I would pay to see that, actually."

"With my luck, I'd break my hand and his nose would be fine," said Nicole.

"Who said you'd have to be the one to do it?"

"Who would do it—you?"

"Not necessarily," Diane replied.

"Then who?"

"I don't know. We could find someone. How hard could it be?"

"Oh, yeah. We'd do really well in the hit-man business. There isn't anyone. You know why? 'Cause everyone loved him," Nicole said, swallowing down the last of her piña colada.

A thought entered Diane's head as though someone inside her brain switched on a light bulb. Fighting against the effects of her third Coors, she navigated her words carefully in Nicole's direction.

"Do you… remember… that time… we were in McDonald's… and Garrett arm wrestled John… for the last French fry?"

"Oh my God, yes… stupid."

"And their fists came down like *BANG*… on the edge of the tray? And the whole thing flipped over? And Curtis—Curtis had chocolate shake awwhhhhllll over his pants?"

"There was even milkshake on his eyebrows," recalled Nicole.

"I know! But he didn't know it—that there was shake on his face, too. And that's why Garrett and John couldn't stop laughing. 'Cuz he didn't know it."

The girls' laughter drew attention from the other customers in the Bobcat, including the mismatched couple on the blind date, who welcomed the distraction.

"Who even won that stupid arm wrestle?" asked Nicole.

"I don't remember."

"Wait—John did!"

"How do you remember that? All I remember is milkshake flying evvvvvreeeewherrrr," Diane motioned with a circular sweep of her outstretched arm.

"Yes, yes, yes, yes, yes, yes, yes! Don't you remember?" Nicole insisted, banging her fist multiple times on the counter, drawing increased attention from customers. "It was John, because the next thing you know, he was on his hands and knees on the floor looking all over to see where the French fry went. He was determined to eat it."

Diane's face turned suddenly glum.

"Well, don't be all sad about it. Why are you sad all of a sudden?" Nicole asked her friend.

"I'm not sad."

"Then, what?"

"It's way more serious than that." Diane appeared as though she might cry.

"What do you mean?"

"But, if I tell you, you can't laugh, Nicole. You have to promise you won't laugh at me. "

Nicole steadied her gaze at Diane. "Okay, you're scaring me. What's going on? Tell me."

"I don't—I can't—remember where I parked."

Nicole tried hard to swallow a chuckle. "Why would I laugh?"

"See, I knew you would laugh!" Diane accused.

"Sorry. You're right, it's not funny."

"Noooo, it's not. Because, listen. Because it's stupid, Nicole. Think about it."

"It's not stupid. You're just drunk."

"Yeah, it is."

"No, it's not. It's stupid that you're sad about it, Di," Nicole said affectionately.

"Are you calling me stupid?"

"No, you called you stupid."

"No, I didn't,"

"Yes, you did," replied Nicole.

"Oh, wait. Maybe I did. You know what? I want to propose a toast."

"Okay! To what?"

Diane held up her beer and beamed. Nicole picked up her nearly empty piña colada glass. "To the bright and sunny future ahead and to knowing you're gonna be okay!"

Tonight's laughter had felt good, partly because it was shared with Diane, and partly because it massaged the wound left by Garrett that, until this reunion with her best friend, Nicole was certain would kill her.

Chapter Twenty-Five

Hurt So Bad
Linda Rondstadt, 1980

The multi-colored bricks supporting the walls of the ancient Anglican church on the outskirts of Mississauga held nearly two centuries worth of background stories surrounding events like today's. It was a perfect afternoon for an autumn wedding, not sunny, but not cloudy, and not windy (which was atypical for this time of year) yet breezy enough to release one's thoughts into the breeze, if one wanted to get rid of one's thoughts.

Diane was kind enough to bring Nicole along as her 'plus one,' but it hadn't been without Garrett's approval. "I'm glad he doesn't mind if I come," Nicole had said, secretly hoping her presence at Garrett's wedding had incited at least an intense, twenty-four hour debate between him and his fiancée, or in the best case scenario, one that lasted two or three days. What she couldn't bear was the thought that whether or not Nicole came to the wedding may have warranted little or no conversation at all.

Small groups of festively dressed guests carried their chit-chat from the beautifully manicured courtyard to the inside of the church.

"Guess it's that time," Diane whispered.

Nicole grabbed another glass of champagne from an unattended tray of full ones on a nearby table. She quickly gulped it down. Once inside the church vestibule, there was nowhere to deposit the empty glass. A waiter at a Manhattan wedding would have been ready and waiting to take it from her the instant it left her lips. To just leave it somewhere, even if she could find a place, was extremely tacky, so instead she hung onto it. Except for the judgmental stare coming from an under-dressed, overly made-up, seventeen-year-old girl whose choice to chew gum on this particular occasion forfeited any right the teenager had to judge Nicole, surely no one would notice.

The effect of the bubbly stuff threatened to sabotage Nicole's efforts to focus on the pattern in the tweed suit that encased the woman seated directly in front of her. The design was a delicate weave of mauve and cocoa and harvest gold and Nicole wanted to climb inside the silky threads and be enveloped by all of them. The woman was most likely an aunt or something of Garrett's. She was petite and classy and feminine and her body language, along with the giddy way she whispered to the guest seated next to her, telegraphed an infectious personality that told Nicole she had to be in the bloodline—not just a family friend.

Nicole wanted to tap this lovely individual on the shoulder so she would turn around to reveal a face as glorious and wise as Nicole imagined. Then Nicole would ask her, "What do I do? I'm in love with the groom and we belong together and this is all wrong. This whole day is wrong. It's not the script I wrote for my life, and if I'd been paying attention, maybe I could have changed it. But I was stupid and now it's too late and if I lose him, I'm going to die right here in this seat and no one will know why. Not even him. I can't die before he at least knows the truth. Help me."

A string quartet began to play the Wedding Song and everyone rose to their feet. The music choice had to have been the bride's. Garrett would have chosen a far less traditional piece, such as *Wachet Auf, Cantata No. 140* by Bach, or Mozart's Minuet from *Don Giovanni*. In all fairness, the female in the wedding gown making her way down the aisle was quite radiant. But weren't all brides radiant on their wedding day? Her dress was beautiful but understated, a simple, white satin A-line with a modest train. The bodice was fitted, showing off a curvaceous figure, which, Nicole realized, was completely unclothed the first and only other time Nicole had seen it. Walking a few paces in front of the formerly-known-as Sudsy Visitor, was an adorable cherub of a girl carrying a small white basket, invoking an audible sigh of delight from the crowd with every fist-full of pink rose petals her tiny hand released to the floor.

"Just focus on the cute little girl," Nicole told herself. "Don't focus on Pamela—Paulina—what's her name."

Had Nicole really blocked out her name? Why couldn't she remember it? Was it the champagne?

Her name didn't matter anyway. What mattered was that Garrett was waiting for her at the end of the aisle.

Nicole imagined how handsome he must look standing there, his captivating blue eyes taking it all in, feeling genuine gratitude for the people who'd come to share this special time in his life. He was, no doubt, somewhat uncomfortable in the suit he was wearing, which Nicole sensed was more deep charcoal than black, and though his palms may be sweaty, his posture telegraphed that he was calm and in control. Nicole could only guess at these things because if she looked at Garrett and saw something—anything—resembling a glow from inside him that could be true love for this girl about to stand at his side, it would leave Nicole unable to breathe.

The officiant asked that they all be seated. *Thank God*, Nicole thought. She had begun to feel queasy.

Nicole's mind drifted. She thought of the countless times she'd fantasized about this scene, when she was the one Garrett would turn to face. He'd find her breathtaking, more beautiful than he'd ever seen her, and they'd be so caught up in the miracle—that their lives really were intended to be joined together forever—that the bond between them would be felt by everyone in the room. Isn't that the way it had all started? She remembered the first time she saw him, then the first time she kissed him, then the first time they spent the night together and how waking up next to him was the one thing in her life she knew would always feel right. So none of what was happening right now made sense except the words Nicole heard next.

"Do you who are assembled here support this union and affirm that these two should be married today?"

The crowd uttered an affectionate, "We do."

And then it happened. Just like in the movies. Nicole wasn't sure how the sound left her body, but she opened her mouth and a deliberate "No" came out. There was a collective gasp from the wedding guests and all heads turned in Nicole's direction, speculating where the objection had come from. Perhaps she should stand up, she thought. She had brought the ceremony to a screeching halt, and if she were going to run the risk of Garrett and his family—his dear family, who had extended nothing but love to the bright, beautiful, outgoing girl from Wishton who had stolen the heart of the new boy from out of town—labeling her a despicable human being, she may as well own it. In what seemed to take the time it took to read Homer's Iliad, Nicole's knees lifted her to a standing position.

"No, I can't support this union. It's wrong. I'm sorry, but it is… You can't do this, Garrett. You can't tell this lie. I mean, you can go through with it if you want to, but not before I tell the truth. And Paula, I know how much you must hate me right now and what a horrible human being you think I am for doing this, and you're probably a very nice person—in fact, I know you're a very nice person because Garrett wouldn't have chosen you if you weren't—but you deserve a man who really loves you and wants to spend the rest of his life with you. Not a man who—who's marrying you in order to forget someone else."

Nicole didn't know which was worse: when a 104 fever from a nearly ruptured spleen brought on by mono caused her to tank in the middle of her most important audition at Carnegie, or the spotlight garnered by the monologue she was delivering at this moment.

"… Someone who maybe forgets sometimes that people make mistakes. Someone who's far from perfect herself, in fact, perfectly flawed in a lot of ways. That's what you used to say, remember? You told me when we were in high school that what made me perfect was that I was perfectly flawed, or my flaws were perfect, or something weird like that, that you said. And see, I love you too much to let you ruin three lives today, Garrett. Don't ruin your life and her life and my life. Don't do it."

Nicole couldn't look directly at Garrett's face. Knowing the pain she'd inflicted upon Paula, she couldn't bring herself to look at her, either. The expressions on the faces of the wedding guests made Nicole feel not just evil, but dirty. Diane, who agreed to let Nicole come with her, looked at her friend with equal parts disgust and distrust. With nowhere to look but down, and nothing to feel but pathetic, Nicole picked up the pink velvet clutch Garrett had given her for her 17th birthday, eased past the folks seated in her row, and walked out of the little church at the edge of Mississauga.

Chapter Twenty-Six

Love Don't Live Here Anymore
Madonna, 1996

I lifted my hands away from the keyboard and leaned back in the chair. I stared at the computer screen, feeling little satisfaction in allowing my heroine to behave so selfishly. It was certainly not something I could have done. Or could I? If it had been Liam, would I have had the courage to do such a thing?

My gaze remained fixed on the monitor. Should I rewrite that chapter? Was Nicole a despicable human being for trying to stop Garrett's wedding? Would Nicole have even gone? No, no and yes. I could think of worse things than interrupting a wedding, like running out of food at the reception or having a mix-up with the floral delivery that resulted in no flowers, including the bridal bouquet. I couldn't bring myself to rewrite that part any more than Nicole could've sat through the excruciating ceremony without doing something.

Nicole wasn't a despicable person. She'd been despicably hurt and now she was despicably lost without her

Garrett. She never thought about what life would be like without him and she was barely coping. And absolutely, she would have gone to the wedding if Garrett had said it was okay. Furthermore, if Garrett and Paula were meant to be together, nothing would come between them. Nicole may have ruined their special day, but married people knew weddings were only celebrations that took months to plan, and less than twenty-four hours to experience. Marriage, on the other hand, well, marriage was something else entirely.

Even at its best, marriage could be a mystery. That marriage was a commitment and a partnership that required compromise, and all the things our mothers warned us about, was not where the mystery lie. The mystery was how something that begins as a journey embarked by two people, can transform itself along the way into an unrecognizable foundation beneath their feet, leaving the travelers baffled and confused not only by where they've ended up, but how it was that at one time, they determined with impeccable certainty that the other was intended to walk beside them.

"Why do you feel the need to speak?" Neil had asked me yesterday when we fought. It was the question out of his mouth so many times over the last five years. For a while, it just made me angry, just a symptom of a man who didn't want to be bothered. But it was becoming increasingly clear that if there really were such a thing as a magic wand, Neil wished he had one that would make me disappear.

"Your problem is, you just want to be left alone!" I'd attacked back.

"It's not that I want to be left alone. I just want to be left alone by *you*," he shouted.

Though I'd never said the words out loud, I had to confess that I, too, had felt the same way once. Over the years, it would become what I nicknamed *The Savannah Phrase*.

***

My younger sister, Cassandra, after whom I named my daughter, enjoyed a comfortable living in Georgia, with her husband, Tony. She taught chemistry at one of the local high schools and Tony was an instructor at The Savannah School of Art and Design. The reason I named Cassandra after my sister was not because my sister and I were particularly close. I mean, we were in some respects, but I did it because my sister was the one who did everything right.

Born three years ahead of her, I was the older one who was supposed to set an example for my baby sister. Instead, I was a chatterbox kid whose mouth was always getting me into trouble, including a couple visits to the principal's office for sharing my unsolicited suggestions to the teacher on how to run her class. As for my interests, I was a 'Jack of all trades and master of none,' unsure of where my true passions lay because I loved all of them equally. I started dance lessons at four, piano lessons at six, not long after that I was drawn to performing and never missed an audition for the school play.

In high school I joined Key Club and Art Club and Debate Club and Coin Club, and by senior year I was editor of the school newspaper. Except for athletics, an area in which my below average skills were a waste of everyone's time, including my own, I was involved in just about everything. When it was time for me to attend college, I struggled with choosing a major. Theatre sounded exciting and wonderful but journalism drew me like an irresistible lover whom one will risk anything to be with. Somehow theatre won the coin toss for college major and the writer inside me stepped quietly to the back of the bus, rejected, disrespected and confused.

My sister, on the other hand, knew from the moment she was born that she wanted to be a teacher, a chemistry teacher of all things. I say 'of all things,' because there was no way my creatively tormented mind could ever grasp science, let alone teach it to someone else. But Cassandra adored science. She had one of those brains that loved formulas and equations and figuring out how organisms worked.

The only item that strayed outside the lines of Cassandra's perfectly sensible goals was that, interestingly, she married an artist. I always knew there was a lover of art somewhere deep inside Cassandra. She couldn't very well avoid it after all the years I forced her to sit still and be my audience of one, while I performed skits in our basement. But I never pictured her married to an illustrator. Unlike me, Tony had succeeded in finding a specific focus for his creative expression, one that fulfilled him and filled his pockets at the same time. My parents loved that about him.

When the movie *Midnight in the Garden of Good and Evil* was being filmed on location in Savannah, the script supervisor, who was a friend of my sister's, mentioned that the crew needed a temporary replacement to assist on script because her assistant had suffered an emergency appendectomy. Cassandra immediately thought of my love for the creative process—*any* creative process—and how jazzed I would be to have an opportunity to work with a famous director like Clint Eastwood.

"I told her your obsession with detail was enough to make anyone crazy but what sold her is that your actual day job is you're a proofreader. The job is yours if you want it. How fast can you get here?" my sister had said.

While I was trying to contain my excitement, she went on to say, "And Tony and I will be in Australia and New Zealand on vacation, so you and Neil will have the entire place to yourself. You guys can run around naked and do it anywhere in the house you want! It'll be like a second honeymoon. Mom can keep the kids."

My mother did volunteer to keep Cassandra and Sean, who were eight and six at the time. I insisted that Neil come with me because the three week commitment would mean being away on our wedding anniversary. I could think of nothing more perfect than combining this exciting opportunity with a romantic getaway for the two of us. But Neil was not as excited as I was by the idea. In fact, Neil wasn't excited at all.

"But you love Savannah," I pleaded. "And Cassandra and Tony will be gone. We'll have the whole place to ourselves!"

"I don't love Savannah."

"What do you mean? You didn't have a good time last Christmas?"

"I had a good time at Christmas but it's not as if we saw any of Savannah. We hung out at your sister's most of the time and the two of you went last minute Christmas shopping while me and Tony tried to hear the football game while the kids were at each other's throats," Neil said as he kicked off his Reeboks and settled into the Lazy Boy recliner. Then he reached for his paperback novel, apparently finished with the discussion.

I walked over to where he was sitting and pressed my hand gently on the inside of his elbow, preventing him from lifting the book to read.

"This is important to me," I said.

"Of course it is. Everything you want to do is important to you."

"That's not fair."

"I can see you've decided to go, no matter what."

"It's our anniversary. Please come with me?"

Four days later my mom arrived to stay with the kids for what we knew would be a glorious time filled more with opportunities to spoil them, rather than making sure they got their homework done and got to bed early. Even though I knew they were in safe and loving hands, it was never easy to say goodbye to my children, and this trip would be the longest time I'd ever been away from them.

Neil said very little during the fifty minute ride to the airport. To fill the uncomfortable silence, I read portions out loud from a tour book I'd ordered about Savannah.

"What do you think about taking one of those ghost tours? There's so much haunted history and cool stories that are part of the culture there. And Cassandra said she left a list of restaurants that we absolutely have to try."

I looked over at Neil to see if I'd elicited any kind of response. I hadn't. Something was definitely up and for the first time since this whole thing was discussed, I was seriously concerned that he was going to behave like this the entire time we were in Savannah. We eased into the Departures Only lane at LAX, but instead of parking the car in the long term lot as we'd talked about the night before, Neil pulled over to the curb just in front of Delta Airlines and stopped.

"What are you doing?" I asked.

He reached into the inside breast pocket of his Dockers jacket and pulled out our plane tickets, and handed them to me. The barely audible sigh he made was the kind that precedes something the speaker regrets they have to say.

"I'm not going."

I was unprepared for the blow his announcement sent to my stomach. It was a strange kind of hurt. I was literally being kicked to the curb by the person who was supposed to love me the most.

"What?" was the only word I could manage. Then, "Why?"

"This is not about us or our anniversary. It's about you."

"Well, okay, yeah, the job is about me, but so what? I don't understand why you're doing this. How could you just dump me out like this?"

The sting from the wound he inflicted made its way down through my hips and legs and permeated through my feet. I realized I was shaking and for a moment I wasn't sure my body would have the strength to get out of the car. The feeling engulfed me, and found its way back into my chest. I could feel my tears ready to follow.

"Have a good time. I'll tell your mom we had a change of plans but she can certainly hang out as long as she wants. We'll see you in three weeks."

His words were not angry, not cold. They were a simple, direct delivery of necessary information, much like a newscast. And there was no time for a discussion because I had a plane to catch, which had to be part of his reason for telling me this at the precise moment that he did.

***

My three weeks in Savannah turned out to be very different from what I had planned.

It was almost 6:30 p.m. on the second day of my brand new job as an assistant script supervisor. I'd been forced to learn fast and used every shred of experience I had to make my sister proud. Living in Los Angeles, I knew a little bit about the motion picture business and that everyone on a set had a very specific job to do, but the only way to describe it all was simply, *amazing*.

"Hey, new girl! Amanda? Is that your name?" a male voice shouted.

"It's Miranda," I smiled, turning around to find the voice among ten different bodies all very involved in moving things from around the place where I was standing.

"Sorry. Miranda. We've gotta strike this area. Can you stand somewhere else?"

"Sure, okay."

Just as I stepped to my left to avoid a nine foot Greek statue made of Styrofoam on a dolly headed straight towards me, something that felt like a heavy rubber snake wrapped around my ankles and yanked my feet out from under me. At the same moment, the clipboard and spiral notebook I was holding went flying into the air and my body hit the concrete.

***

When I came to seven hours later, I was in a hospital bed in downtown Savannah, surrounded by two surgeons and a physician's assistant.

"Well, hi, there."

The words came from a mouth on a head attached to a male body dressed from head to toe in a light shade of foam green. I was very sleepy and realized there were some serious drugs at work.

"Do you know where you are and what happened to you?"

I knew I was in Savannah and not Los Angeles, but all I cared about at the moment was the intense pain that was shooting through my right hand and up my arm, which was encased in a cast and attached to some kind of metal mechanism dangling above the bed.

"Hurts," I frowned.

"Okay, we're about to give you another dose of morphine, don't worry. Then you'll be on something lighter. Can you tell us your name and where you are?"

"Miranda Peterson… I'm in Savannah helping on that movie. I think I fell."

"You certainly did. You tripped over a big fat cable and decided to break your fall with your arm."

The other two figures listened intently while Foam Green and I continued our little get-to-know fest.

"You broke two fingers, and fractured all three puppies in your right arm."

"All three what?" I asked.

"Your ulna and radius, and a piece of the humerus. You fractured all three. So we're guessing you're the kind of gal that doesn't do anything half way. Oh, and you've got a little hairline fracture on your collar bone. But that'll take care of itself."

I suddenly felt nauseous. I thought he said when I hit the floor I broke all the bones in my arm and two fingers and a little piece of my collar bone. He had. Tears filled my eyes. One of the silent figures finally spoke. This time it was a female.

"We had to operate to get you back up and running," she said. "You can go home tomorrow but before you do, we want to take another look at you. There's a little bruise on your hip and we want to make sure that's all it is."

"What *isn't* wrong with me?" I mumbled.

"Well, you didn't kill yourself," she grinned. The other two chucked but I failed to find the humor in the statement. Foam Green patted my free hand and the three of them walked out of the room.

I remembered the guy on the crew yelling at me to move out of the way, but not much after that, though the ride in the ambulance was slowly coming back. I had broken the second and third fingers on my right hand, quickly ending my career as a temporary assistant script supervisor, and would be in a cast up to my shoulder for at least two months. The production company was probably starting to wonder if the assistant script supervisor position was jinxed.

***

Cassandra insisted she and Tony end their vacation to come home and look after me. I insisted they do no such thing. They asked if Neil was going to fly out to be with me and they were shocked when I told them he didn't know what happened. I hadn't told him because I simply had no desire to talk to him. Once I accepted the fact that I would have to befriend my left hand if the two of us were ever going to work together to accomplish the tasks I needed to accomplish, I didn't feel any great need for anyone to take care of me, least of all Neil.

I soon mastered the art of showering without getting the cast wet, and once I managed to get the packages opened, which could sometimes take up to five minutes, I could make a few things in the microwave when I was hungry. Working the remote became easier and easier with practice, and I watched more TV than any one person should have been allowed.

It was strange being alone in someone else's space, but I resigned myself to make the best of it, grateful for this period of solitude in the quiet house. The only sound I looked forward to hearing was my children's voices over the phone, which I did every few days. And when I wasn't pumped with vicodin, I made an effort to take in every detail of my environment. The family photographs throughout my sister's home, some of which were of her and me growing up, and the interesting artwork she and Tony had collected through the years, provided a special comfort.

Even the heavy Georgia humidity felt nice on the occasional afternoons I'd venture out onto the back patio. In my concerted effort to give my left arm an occasional break from having to do everything, my thighs and lower legs grew stronger from the repetitive task of slowly lowering myself onto the navy blue cushioned chaise. Once seated, I discovered a way to recline comfortably amid my sister's lush haven of peach trees, and frequently dozed off long enough to wake rejuvenated before having to repeat the maneuver in reverse.

. Neil phoned on our wedding anniversary the following week. Cassandra had given him the broad strokes about my mishap, so I provided a more detailed account. My delivery of the story was similar to the news report he'd given me when he dumped me at the airport, intended only to relay facts.

"Are you sure you don't need me to come out there, Miranda?" If he was hurt that he learned about my accident from my sister, instead of me, he didn't let on.

"I'm sure."

"Okay. Well, you probably want to be left alone, so I'll go. Happy Anniversary."

"Happy Anniversary."

Once I was back home, I yearned for my cast to be off, not only so I'd have the use of my arm back, but so it would no longer be a symbol for what had happened between me and Neil. For me, it stood for his abandonment of me, both physically and emotionally. For him, it was something I'd brought on myself due to my selfishness where his feelings were concerned. The trouble was, though the bones I broke soon healed and went back to normal, Neil and I never were again.

***

A couple years after the Savannah fiasco, Neil made a devastating discovery involving Raymond Churney, Neil's best friend since childhood and partner in the management consulting firm they'd built together from the ground up.

We'd all been ecstatic when Vanwade, a California-based pharmaceutical company, and Neil and Ray's biggest client, offered to bring Neil and Ray on fulltime as in-house consultants. It was a move that would significantly benefit our family and ultimately change our lives. About three weeks before the deal was supposed to close, Neil learned that Ray had gone behind his back and made

a deal with Vanwade under the table that not only ex-
cluded Neil, but reduced the firm's assets by more than
half when Ray walked.

Little by little, Neil rebuilt the company with the help
of a hot shot grad student fresh out of the Business
School at Berkeley, whose brains and skills came at a
lower price than what a seasoned professional would've
cost. But his friend's betrayal and the financial setback it
caused our family nearly destroyed him. It left a nasty
wound that never healed, infecting our already toxic marriage.

***

I just want to be left alone by you.

Though they may have been words spoken in anger,
their meaning held the fabric of our marriage up to the
light and forced me to look at it. I could see the places
where it had grown irreparably thin and the remaining
threads were too weak to survive any further strain. Last
night made too many nights that I'd cried myself to sleep
wondering if it was pride or shame I should feel for becoming accustomed to an empty marriage.

Although I knew divorcing Neil would leave me
drowning in guilt every time I looked into the eyes of my
children, I prayed that someday they could accept that
their parents' journey together had come to an end. I
would make sure they knew their mother still believed
that marriage was a good thing, a special kind of glue ca-
pable of holding some people together forever. But I
didn't need purplish, velvety letters in the mirror to tell
me mine was over.

Chapter Twenty-Seven

That's the Way I've Always Heard It Should Be
Carly Simon, 1971

Garrett scribbled 'Return to Sender' across the envelope and put it back inside the mailbox on the front porch. It was the fourth one he'd returned to Nicole in the last seven months. He'd opened the first one—the one that came right after the wedding. Nothing she could say would take away the hurt that resulted from her selfish behavior that day, but he'd read the letter, just the same.

***

Dear Garrett,

I hope there's a forwarding address where this will reach you. Normally I would have something carefully thought out to say, but in this case, I'm so overwhelmed with regret for what I did that I'll just say what I feel. First of all, I know you hate me. And I know that 'sorry' can't take back what I did. I was sincerely grateful that you told Diane I could come as her guest, and I didn't set out to cause trouble. Something came over me while the minister was talking. It was like my whole life was flashing before my eyes or something and all I could think about was how much I loved you and how this whole thing you were doing was a big mistake. I should have been thinking about how lucky Paula was and how happy I should be for the two of you but I just couldn't.

I know I pushed you away and stopped taking your calls after you moved out. That was my fault. When I found out you were getting married, I felt like my whole life was over. And I know she was just a rebound for you. If that sounds mean, I'm sorry. It's just that I'll never understand how you could fall in love with someone else so quickly, Garrett, let alone get married. It's so difficult to accept. What I did was a despicable thing to do, but what about our motto that you only live once? I know I don't have the right to ask this, but please tell Paula that I'm not the horrible person she saw that day. I'm a decent person who did a terrible thing. Tell her something came over me, and I'm so, so sorry. All I can hope for now is that at some point you'll find it in your heart to forgive me.

I have to figure out my life without you now and I don't know how. I guess I never thought it would be your life and my life. I always thought it would be our life. I don't know what else to say. I'm moving back to New York in a few weeks. Please write back and tell me how you're doing. I know our lives are different now, but I couldn't bear the thought of losing touch with you.

All my love,
Nicky

***

Nicole had no idea just how different Garrett's life had become. Life, itself, arrived a month ago in the form of the most beautiful thing Garrett had ever seen. It was perfect, and precious and it made everything else in Garrett's life so far seem unimportant. It was love personified and Garrett could not fathom how he'd been chosen to receive such a miraculous gift. Not only did he feel unworthy, he had absolutely no knowledge of what to do with the amazing creature now that it was here. Paula, however, seemed to have some natural connection with the tiny thing from the moment she looked into its eyes, and the bond was breathtaking to observe. But Garrett would have something in common with the extraordinary little being that Paula would never have. It was male. And they named him Taylor.

Chapter Twenty-Eight

I Can't Make You Love Me
Bonnie Raitt, 1991

Taylor Matthew McKinnon, now six months old, was one of those adorably scrumptious, chubby cheeked babies with perfectly round, piercing blue eyes he'd been gifted from his father. A good natured baby, he was so quiet that folks frequently failed to realize he was in the room. It was the same way this morning. From the comfort of his baby carrier, pacifier firmly secure in his mouth, little Taylor stared at his mom's sullen face as the two of them occupied a quiet corner of the empty chapel. It was cold inside the sanctuary and Paula regretted not bringing a sweater. Taylor, however, was snug and warm inside the powder blue angora blanket that Paula's mom had knitted for him, with whimsical figures of navy blue African elephants woven throughout.

Fifteen minutes had already passed while Paula's eyes dedicated themselves to discerning the details in the massive stained glass window. There were ten stained glass windows in all, five on one side of the chapel and five on the other. Each portrayed a parable from the Bible and the one that captivated her attention today was the Parable of the Sower. The story depicts a sower whose seed falls upon four kinds of ground. The hard ground represents someone who is hardened by sin, who hears, but does not understand God's word. The stony ground represents one who professes delight with God's word, but when trouble arises, his faith disappears. The thorny ground stands for someone whose heart is captivated by the riches of the world, leaving him no time for the word of God; and the fertile ground represents the person who hears, understands, and allows the word of God to accomplish results in his life.

Paula wanted very much to be the fertile, yielding soil that stays open to the teachings of Christ, but what she needed today was a sign, or something, that would tell her what to do. Though nothing could have prepared her for the role of motherhood, she accepted it as the consequence for failing to keep the level head that might have prevented her from having unprotected sex. The truth of the matter was, if she could go back to the moment she met Garrett McKinnon, she wouldn't change a thing.

But now, there was a deeper meaning behind Garrett's behavior that she couldn't ignore anymore. She wanted an end to the conversation she kept having with herself that she was *just being silly*. How long could she bury her sadness at hearing Nicole's name from Garrett's lips while he slept? A few dreams were one thing. She, too, might have occasionally uttered the name of an ex-boyfriend in her sleep, if she had ever had an ex-boyfriend.

But she'd never seriously dated anyone before the irresistible chap who walked into the coffee shop that morning back in New York. Paula believed Garrett loved her, but it was different from the way she longed to be loved by him. She wanted to be the object of the comment she heard him make last night. It was the most disturbing one so far.

"I'll always love you, Nicole… Where are you? Come back to me." The words had made Paula so nauseous that she worried whether Taylor might be affected when she breastfed him this morning.

The door at the rear of the church made a soft squeak, and a robust woman who appeared to be the wedding coordinator entered carrying a huge roll of white satin ribbon and a gargantuan pair of scissors. She strode purposefully to the front of the chapel and set about her decorating duties without noticing the young woman and her baby seated in the back.

Paula looked down at Tay, as he was nicknamed, his doll-like eyes still unwavering from his mother's face.

"Your father's a good guy. But he's still in love with her. And I don't know how long it's going to take till he's not in love with her anymore. And I don't know what to do."

She didn't want to start crying, especially now that she wasn't alone in the church. She wiped a tear from her eye the instant it threatened to fall. Mirroring his mother's emotion, Taylor's face began to contort into a confused sadness. Seeing her baby's pain, Paula quickly forced a smile.

"But he loves you more than he'll ever love anything. Who wouldn't? Have you seen you?"

Taylor cooed softly and returned his mother's ear to ear grin, forcing the pacifier to drop out of his mouth, only to be caught by Paula before it tumbled to the cold wood floor. She dropped the pacifier in her purse, picked up the baby carrier with one hand and anchored the strap of her purse to the opposite shoulder with the other. Then mother and son walked out of the church into the far less peaceful world waiting outside.

Chapter Twenty-Nine

Sara Smile
Hall and Oates, 1975

Garrett purged his mailbox of unwanted emails as he customarily did every morning the moment he arrived at work. Resuming a position at de Havilland after being away for a while to live in New York could not have been a better stroke of luck. He was a husband and father now, and baby food didn't come cheap. What's more, he loved his job. If only they had a piano somewhere in the building that he could tickle when he was on a break. That would make this already stimulating environment truly heaven on earth.

Garrett found this new trend of computer electronic mail extremely convenient. It made communication much faster than regular mail, and Garrett was certain it wouldn't be long before it would take the place of traditional correspondence altogether. What was bothersome was that folks had scarcely gotten used to the idea before it was already finding a way to send customers unsolicited crap. Two offers for an oil change on his car, an invitation to buy life insurance, and a response from some travel agency claiming to confirm an upcoming trip, were the items to be trashed this morning. He saved one of the two oil change coupons and the other one—*Delete*. He felt too young to think about life insurance though he probably should be. *Delete*. He had no idea what a travel agency could be following up with him about, so he clicked on it. It was for some spiritual retreat in Spain he and Nicole looked into after a two hour discussion they had one night about the soul's ability to reach a higher level of consciousness. Nicole had thought the trip was a great idea, and, as usual, whenever she thought something was a great idea, there was no talking her out of it. *Delete*.

It was 9:53. Garrett straightened his tie and grabbed the report he'd prepared for the 10:00 department meeting. It was his first company presentation and it felt good, for once, to contribute more than just the grunt work. He tried hard not to let his nerves get the best of him, but it felt like the nerves were winning. Public speaking wasn't his forte, but luckily humor was. He'd start with a joke to break the ice, and once the entire room was reduced to laughter, he'd have his audience in the palm of his hand. After that, if they still noticed how terrified he was, they wouldn't care.

Hidden in his desk drawer was a little cosmetic mirror that always came in handy when he needed to make sure there was nothing stuck in his teeth. He did a quick check of his smile, popped up from his chair and walked briskly down the hallway. Garrett always turned left when he walked out of his cubicle. Even though it was the longer way to the board room and everything else in the office, it was the opposite direction from Tanya, the girl in the cubicle to his right. Tanya reminded him of Nicole. She was beautiful and smart, with a feisty personality that masked her insecurities. If that weren't enough to evoke memories of Nicole, Tanya's face, figure and even body rhythm resembled Nicole's, too. Garrett had a reputation for being the funny guy in the office who was nice to everyone, and he hoped Tanya didn't notice what pains he took to avoid her. A man had to do what a man had to do and he didn't need his heart broken by a daily encounter with Nicole's clone.

Garrett made his way into the board room with the other staff members and took one of the sixteen seats around the long, glass table. He feigned interest in the two presentations before his, and focused only on the moment it was time for him to walk to the front of the room.

"Before I get started, I just want to say, there's a saying that if you're nervous to speak in front of people, just picture them in their underwear. I'm not sure how that's supposed to help, but you all look great in yours."

Laughter surrounded the table.

"Rob, I'm afraid you don't look as good in your underwear as Marcie does in hers, but no surprise there, I'm sure."

More laughter and a sudden, deep pink hue flushing Marcie's face.

"Okay. Where our global customer base is concerned, all major engine and airframe OEMs, as well as Tier 1 and 2 suppliers to the engines, have remained solid, with this quarter's figures rivaling last quarter. However, with Tier 3s, we're a little short on the numbers we had last quarter.

If we can get some of them back, we'll still be one of the top five supporters internationally of MRO and aircraft operators with repair and overhaul capabilities…"

Garrett's palms stung from all the high-fives he received from his co-workers throughout the rest of the afternoon. He was proud of the job he'd done and was anxious to tell Paula how it went. He felt something inside him gently close that door between being an awkward rookie and possessing the self-confidence that comes from *knowing that you know*. Somewhere in that *knowing that you know* space, there's always room for arrogance to reside. But if the space is filled with enough things made from materials that have value, arrogance will find the surroundings too uncomfortable to want to stay for more than a short period of time.

There was no answer when he'd called Paula earlier this morning. He didn't remember her saying she had to go out today, but with a baby at home, there was no telling what could arise. They had worked out a system where Garrett took the train to work every day, leaving Paula with the car. It was the same Pontiac he'd had since high school. On the short list of things they needed, a new car was near the top. But for the time being, thank goodness the Pontiac still ran great.

It was 5:00. Garrett jumped up from his cubicle and joined the throngs of other de Havilland employees heading out to the parking lot. Just outside the exit door, to his surprise, was Paula.

"Hey!" Garrett said, giving her a squeeze.

"Hi."

"What are you doing here? Is everything okay? Where's Tay?"

"He's in the car. Everything's fine. We're fine." Paula gestured toward a parked vehicle Garrett didn't recognize. The woman in the driver's seat was Paula's friend, Catherine, another young mom who lived in their neighborhood.

A quizzical frown crawled across Garrett's brow. "What's going on?"

"Cathy's giving me a ride to my mum's."

"Did something happen to the car?"

"No. The car's at home," Paula replied.

"Um, okay. But that's two hours. You'll be getting back so late."

"I'm not coming back tonight."

That's weird, Garrett thought. But so far this whole conversation had been a little weird, so he just kept up his part of the Q&A in the hope that something would add up.

"So you'll wait till tomorrow morning, then?"

Paula glanced down at the pavement, and then looked around. When she did that, Garrett knew there was more to this discussion than transportation logistics.

"I just need to get away for a little bit."

Garrett took a moment to digest the announcement.

"But, why?"

"I think… I'm worried that you have some unresolved feelings."

"Unresolved feelings?"

"Yah."

"About what?"

"About Nicole."

Garrett failed to see how the timing of this topic was appropriate, while the motor—in desperate need of oil, his ears determined—was running in a car about to take away his wife and son.

"All right. I mean—what?" he asked.

"So, you agree?"

"No, of course, I don't agree! I agree that's what you apparently think. And I can't believe you came all the way down here to discuss it. You really want to talk about this now?"

"I'd rather not talk about it at all, Garrett."

"Well, that's hardly fair, eh?"

"Well, it was better than leaving you a note. I didn't think that would be right."

"Thanks. How big of you."

"You talk in your sleep, Garrett."

"Let me just make sure I understand. You're running off to your mum's because I talk in my sleep?"

"Of course not."

"Then, I don't understand."

"You talk in your sleep about *her*. All the time."

"So what?"

"Begging her to come back."

"You can't be serious, Paulie?"

"That's pretty serious, to me."

As it always did this time of day, the temperature was dropping steadily, extending no gratitude to the couple as their bodies became aware of the increasing chill in the September air.

"Paula, Nicole and I have known each other since we were sixteen. I'm sure there are plenty of subconscious memories of her in my head. You've gotta cut me a little slack."

"But deep down inside, I think you may still have feelings for her. And it's not just in your sleep. When you stare off into space or when you're quiet and get this weird look on your face sometimes, I know you're thinking about her."

Paula's demeanor turned incredibly calm, indicating a solid confidence that she had an argument that held weight, the kind where you're secure in knowing you've thoroughly researched the facts and examined all the evidence, but the kind where you derive little satisfaction in being right.

The tenderness Garrett was born with swam to the surface and pulled him in a direction he hoped might meet his wife half way.

"Look, love, I'll admit I think of her now and then, but, c'mon, Paula, this is nuts. You're saying I don't pay attention to you and Tay, that I'm not present, or something?"

"No, it's not that. It's… I think you love us—"

"You *think*?"

"I know—you love us."

"Then why are you running off?"

"I just think…" Paula tilted her head affectionately to one side, the way an adult might do when delivering difficult news to a child struggling to accept what he's hearing. "She's *in* there," she whispered gently.

"I don't know what you want me to say," Garrett replied.

"I've gotta go."

"When are you coming back?"

"I'll just be gone a little while."

"What's a little while?"

"I don't know, couple weeks?"

"You're taking Tay and disappearing for a couple weeks?"

"Garrett, please! I don't know, okay? Maybe not that long, maybe only a week. I don't know. I just need some time to think." Paula started back toward her friend's car, Garrett trailing directly behind her.

"Well, it sucks, what you're doing," he protested.

Catherine offered Garrett a monotone, "Hi."

The dull punch Paula had delivered to his stomach forfeited any effort he typically made at basic social politeness so he answered simply, "Unlock the back, please."

Garrett opened the car door and leaned over the sleeping baby. "Hey, little guy. Stay out of trouble, okay?"

"Please don't wake him," Paula whispered from the front seat.

Garrett kissed his son on the forehead and, out of habit, pulled sharply on the straps of the carrier to double check that Taylor was safely locked in. He closed the car door and watched as the vehicle turned out of de Havilland's parking lot and disappeared down the street. For another moment he stood there, trying to decide whether it mattered much if he missed the train home.

Chapter Thirty

Fly Away
Lenny Kravitz, 1998

To go, to get away, to heal, there's nothing more beneficial after someone breaks your heart. Just like the Sting song, we really are 'fragile.' But we can't run from every problem, especially the ones that result from falling in love, or we'd be running all our lives. I'd watched my parents go through trials and tribulations throughout their lives, heard stories about ones they'd been through long before I came along, even. Adding to their stories the things I'd experienced in my own life, I eventually understood the adage, 'What doesn't kill you, makes you stronger.' It was a true statement and I wanted my kids to get it very early. Concerned that the phrase 'what doesn't kill you' might be a little severe for the ears of a four year old, I would always soften it by saying, "Mommy knows that what happened to you hurts a lot right now, but in just a little while, it's going to stop hurting and you're going to feel better, just like when the doctor gives you medicine. First you feel a little bit okay, then soon you feel so much better it's like you were never sick." Not sure how much they bought it. They came out of my body pretty bright.

***

Paula was hurting and she decided she needed to get away to think. Hopefully she'd return with greater clarity about her relationship with Garrett and what, if anything, she should do about their marriage. I wasn't sure yet how things were going to turn out between the two of them. Like all the characters in my book, I would try to let Paula lead me.

Nicole, too, was in need of a new pair of glasses through which she could look at her life. Her break-up with Garrett made me recall the first serious break-up I experienced with a boy I'd fallen deeply in love with just after college. I'm not sure how our romance survived the challenges of my struggle to find work in the entertainment business while he suffered through the unforgiving rigor of medical school, but somehow it had. The concept of marriage started to enter our conversations, beautiful scenes of a future together started to splash onto our canvas. Nothing and no one could convince us we wouldn't last forever, although there were a half dozen signs to the contrary. When it ended after three years, I thought someone had removed my access to oxygen. I was down on the ground and wanted to stay there, and I could see no reason to get back up, knowing that when I did, I wouldn't recognize the world without him in it. All I wanted to do was run away somewhere, but there was still

205

my career to chase and rent to pay and the big 'City of the Angels' to conquer before it conquered me. There were no Tibetan mountain peaks or tranquil huts in Bora Bora for me to escape to, either of which sounded like the perfect antidote.

Nicole was split in two, too. And my heart was breaking for her. I couldn't rescue her, but I'd heard of a wonderful place where I could send her.

Chapter Thirty-One

Come Sail Away
Styx, 1977

Nicole struggled to ignore her jitters as the pilot announced they were beginning their descent into Madrid. A woman she met on a plane a couple years ago told her that if she rested her feet on the metal bar behind the seat in front of her, instead of putting them directly on the floor, she wouldn't feel the vibration as much. She couldn't remember now if she was supposed to do that upon take-off or landing, but she did remember that it hadn't helped at all. The roar of the landing gear rushed through her body. She relied, as she always did when she flew, on a visualization exercise she picked up from a hypnotherapy class she took once. *Close your eyes and count backwards from 10, becoming deeper and deeper relaxed.*

Nicole squeezed her eyes shut. In another five minutes, they were on the ground. Not too bad, she thought. The next part of her journey, the train ride to Sarria, would take several hours. Hopefully she'd be able to sleep most of the way, which she desperately needed to do. Barely twenty-five-years-old and there were few modes of transportation Nicole enjoyed more than her own imagination. She suspected her distaste for trains— not as great as her distaste for planes—always disappointed Garrett, causing them to take very few of them together. He often teased her about her fear of flying. For him, it was something he adored so much, that one of his goals was to train for his pilot's license, a dream of his since childhood. "I can't help who I am," Nicole always told him.

Most likely it was the crash of American 191 that had changed Nicole's feelings about flying. It was nearly three years ago that she had just landed at O'Hare Airport to visit her friend Stephanie. The two were roommates at Carnegie until Stephanie transferred junior year to the University of Chicago, insisting Nicole come visit before graduation. When Nicole got off the plane, she spotted Stephanie's face in the crowd. At the same moment the girls squealed and exchanged a hug, a pounding thud shook the floor beneath them, accompanied by a deafening clap of thunder. Seconds later, Nicole and Stephanie ran with everyone else in the gate area to the floor-to-ceiling windows where they saw a black plume of smoke reaching hundreds of feet into the sky. The chaotic energy inside the terminal confirmed reports of a DC-10 that crashed just moments after take-off, and the scent of burning fuel from the wreckage could be detected inside the airport as it seeped through the interior walls of the facility.

During the somber, two hour bus ride from O'Hare to Stephanie's apartment, the girls lost count of how many emergency vehicles sped past them in the opposite direction. Later that evening, the two of them spent the night in front of the TV wiping their tears as they watched the news coverage of what was called the single worst air tragedy in U.S. history. The girls learned later that none of the ambulances they'd seen racing to Elk Grove field to rescue survivors among the 273 individuals, had been needed.

***

El Camino de Santiago is a 500-mile trail that crosses from France into northern Spain, and ends at the Cathedral of Santiago de Compostela where the remains of Saint James are said to be buried. The route was heavily traveled during the Middle Ages, but the Black Death, the Protestant Reformation and political unrest in 16th-century Europe led to its decline. At the onset of the 1980s, the El Camino de Santiago was revived by pilgrims from all over the world and now thousands walked the trail annually for health, exercise, religious, or spiritual reasons. There were various routes to choose from, lasting anywhere from one to eight weeks, depending on one's personal choice. Nicole had chosen the one week hike. She was no athlete, and the week-long trail seemed just long enough to stretch her physical as well as spiritual muscles.

Nicole would have six hours on the train to think about everything that had happened. It was now more than a year since she and Garrett had spoken, and it was obvious to anyone paying attention that a part of Nicole had died in the process. She had lost over ten pounds, along with almost all interest in her career, and found little joy in getting up in the morning. Moving back to Wishton for a few months had simply been a remedy for not being able to stay in New York. No matter how big the Big Apple, any remnant of it without Garrett had made it too depressing to remain there. Nicole did have Wishton to thank for one thing, however. If she hadn't gone back, she might never have run into Diane. If she hadn't run into Diane, she might never have found out that Garrett was getting married.

She wondered how he was doing now. She wondered about him every day. She had written, but all her letters had come back except one. She couldn't even be certain whether he—they—were still in Toronto, and she didn't like uncertainty. She liked order and setting goals and making plans. This trip to Santiago was one she and Garrett had planned to take together. It was going to be their search for enlightenment in a crazy world. It had not been the plan for her to take it alone.

Chapter Thirty-Two

Misunderstanding
Genesis, 1980

My seat in the waiting area was now, officially, uncomfortable. In the last two hours, I'd read two magazines, *More* and *People*, from cover to cover, and was about to start the book I'd brought with me. I'd been so absorbed in my writing over the past several months that I'd forgotten how important it was for writers to read, and the book I chose to bring with me, of course, was *Wuthering Heights*. I stood up and stretched my legs, sat down again and started to read. But all I could see on the printed page was a picture of a text from Liam I'd received over a year ago.

LIAM: Wouldn't it be wonderful to see
each other again?

My heart skipped a beat when I read the words. To say that seeing Liam for the first time in three decades was something I wanted more than anything, was more than an understatement. It was such a beautiful notion—wait, wasn't that Liam's phrase? Even the words we used to describe things had begun to echo each other over the course of a year. But had the idea of seeing me moved beyond a beautiful notion towards something he desired? Did he still crave it, like I did? *Love*, *want*, *need*, they'd all been words we'd used to describe our feelings for each other. But somehow the idea of actually touching his cheek, looking into his eyes, having him hold me in his arms, was so overwhelming that when he first brought it up, I hadn't known how to respond. When I did answer, I tried to keep the conversation light so he wouldn't detect the depth of my feelings.

MIRANDA: Yes, it would be more than wonderful.
And if it happened, I can't even promise
that I would have both feet planted firmly
on the ground.

LIAM: Both feet on the ground is a
good place to start.

MIRANDA: You know all the right things
to say, don't you, Liam Kincaid?

LIAM: I love you, Miranda.

Were we in love, again? Or in love, still—like Garrett and Nicole? Garrett and Nicole had something between them that couldn't be denied, and it was turning into a great love story.

"If it's such a great love story, where does that put you and Liam?" asked a female voice.

Wait—did Nicole just speak to me? Well, this was a first! Just like a scene from one of the chapters in my book, I was prepared to simply listen to the dialogue to see where it would lead. The only difference was that somehow, I was the other half of the conversation.

"Who asked *you*?" was the only response I could think of.

"'I love you, Miranda. Always have, always will.' Isn't that what he told you?" Nicole replied.

"Are you mocking me?"

"Of course not. I'm wondering why you doubt what he told you."

"He's told me a lot of things," I said.

"You don't believe him?"

"I don't know."

"Why would he lie to you?"

"I don't know. Maybe he likes pretty words. Maybe he likes saying what I want to hear."

"I don't think that's the case," Nicole replied.

I needed to get the upper hand. I needed to make it clear that I was the one that put ideas in *her* head, not the other way around.

"What do you know? You're a character in a book. You only know what I tell you."

"You're saying I don't have a mind of my own?"

She had a point.

"Well, no. I mean, yes, you have a mind of your own, I guess."

"In fact, I would say I'm on a path towards growth. We'll see how this trip to Spain helps. It will help, right? I'll learn something from it?"

"I can't believe we're having this conversation," I said under my breath.

"I feel like I'm learning something every day."

"Well, that's good, at least," I answered flippantly.

"Don't you? Learn something every day?"

Was I learning anything from all this? *Decide/Do.* Maybe I'd learned a little more about that. I didn't want to get into it.

"I'm really tired."

"Me, too," Nicole sighed.

"You, too? How come?"

"Emotionally exhausted."

I rolled my eyes. "Ha! I'll try to go easier on you."

"I doubt that. Sometimes it feels like you don't have any sympathy for me at all."

"Oh, but I do," I reassured her.

"Then why do I feel so lost?"

"A minute ago you felt like you were growing."

"True."

"Life is about lessons, Nicole, learning from our mistakes. Why should you be any different from anybody else?"

"That's kinda mean."

"It's not mean. It's the way it is. Would you rather have a boring life? Do nothing, learn nothing? Never fall in love?"

"You could help me, if you wanted to. You have all the answers."

"Oh, sweetie. I'm afraid I don't have any of the answers."

"But you're older and wiser."

I immediately adjusted her thinking where that was concerned. "No. I'm just older."

An official-looking group of two men and four women, meticulously dressed in matching uniforms, marched by at a gingerly pace.

"Besides," I continued, "You having all the answers wouldn't make a very interesting novel, now, would it?"

"But I'm the young version of you. Isn't that the premise?" Nicole sounded confused.

"Honestly, I'm not sure what the premise is anymore," I sighed.

"You sound almost as lost as I am."

"Maybe."

"Because the lines have blurred?"

"Not necessarily," I replied.

"Are you sure?"

***

This trip back east was for my Aunt Roberta's 90th birthday. Roberta was both a rock and an angel, and a very wise one. She could read my mind ever since I was a little girl.

"You can't be so sensitive, sweetheart," she'd advise me.

It seemed I'd spent my entire life trying to heed that warning, and for my entire life, failed. Was it such a shortcoming to be overly sensitive? To be the one who could feel the sadness of the saddest person in the room? To be moved by the simplest joy? To be transformed, in one moment, by the connection between you and another human being? Roberta would understand my feelings for Liam. She knew you had to chase your dreams if they were ever going to have a chance at coming true. You had to capture moments that you had no guarantee of getting back. You had to create magic out of the mundane and find love in the most unexpected places if you were to truly experience everything life had to offer.

This attempt to see Liam was about the magic we left in Wishton thirty years ago. It was about the embrace we wanted to share again. It was about the kiss we wanted to feel again, the way we'd imagined it over and over and over. Stealing a moment out of time, even if it was only for a few minutes in the middle of a crowded airport, was what it was about. It was by no means the ideal time to coordinate a rendezvous, but life was too short to not make an attempt. Roberta would have understood that, too.

My brain displayed a screen shot of a conversation from two weeks ago.

LIAM: How nice of you to go celebrate
your aunt. I know the two of you
are very close.

MIRANDA: Thank you. Yes, we are.

LIAM: The reunion's near Buffalo?

MIRANDA: Yeah. On Sunday.

LIAM: Just down the road.

MIRANDA: Oh my goodness, that's right. You're only
two hours from there.

LIAM: About two hours and change.

MIRANDA: I don't fly back until late Wednesday.

LIAM: Meaning?

MIRANDA: Meaning… You're going to make me say it?

LIAM: Yes.

MIRANDA: I would love to see you.

LIAM: I would love to see you, too.
What time does your flight leave?

MIRANDA: 7:26 p.m.

LIAM: I'm guessing you'll be at the airport by
5:00?

MIRANDA: Probably. I mean, I could be there earlier,
if I had to be. Look, I know it's a lot to ask
just for a quick hug.

LIAM: Not the most ideal circumstances.

MIRANDA: I know. But, life is short, right?

LIAM: Right.

MIRANDA: So, what do you think?

LIAM: I think it's a lovely thought.

MIRANDA: Meaning?

LIAM: You're going to make me say it?

MIRANDA: Yes.

LIAM: Could you be there by 4:00?
Enough time for a quick hug and
a really bad expensive meal?

MIRANDA: Seriously?

LIAM: Seriously bad and expensive?
Airport food usually is.

MIRANDA: Please let's do it, Liam! Please say you'll
be there before I get on that plane.

LIAM: I'll be there before you get on that plane.

Chapter Thirty-Three

All I Want
Joni Mitchell, 1970

Sarria was a bustling little town full of interesting sights, sounds and aromas. Nicole climbed the half dozen steps of the Pousada de Portomarin, the little hotel she had booked for one night before starting the hike the next day. The dimly lit lobby was small and inviting. Nicole hoped that what little Spanish she had learned in preparation for the trip would be met with compassion by the front desk manager. Fortunately, he received her dismal efforts at the language with a warm, inviting smile and welcomed her to their beautiful country. She was almost too exhausted to stand up, and with room key in hand all she could think about was a bath, a bed, and a good night's sleep.

At sunrise, a shuttle was waiting outside the Pousada to transport Nicole and fourteen other hotel guests to the first checkpoint of the Camino. Nicole had overslept by a few minutes and scurried to take the last seat next to a young girl who looked about eight years old. The couple in the seat behind them gave a silent nod of approval in the child's direction, letting their daughter know it was safe for Nicole to share the seat.

"Hi," Nicole said with a smile.

The little girl managed a shy grin then quickly looked away. *When it comes to the meaning of life, you're probably the smartest one here*, Nicole thought.

The driver announced that in a few minutes they would be reaching their destination. He encouraged them to leave the stress of their lives behind them, and to prepare for being renewed individuals by the time they reached the Compostela a week from now. Nicole prayed that she would, indeed, be changed. Changed and transformed and filled with greater understanding. She would try to clear her mind in the hope that she'd gain a fresh perspective.

In the soothing rhythm of the shuttle's wheels against the road beneath her, the part of her that was Garrett, that had always been Garrett, that would always be Garrett, wrapped around her like a blanket. She suddenly felt as if she were going to sob. It would be okay if she did, she thought. She could feel a multitude of emotions in the collective energy on the bus. That she should start crying shouldn't be a big deal to anyone.

The shuttle came to a stop.

"When you disembark, follow the road to your right. Peace be with you," the driver said. There was a depth to his kindness that remained with Nicole as she stepped off the bus.

"Thank you," she smiled.

Chapter Thirty-Four

Listen to Your Heart
Roxette, 1989

*Y*ou're a grown-up, I told myself. *So be a grown-up and accept the way things turned out.* No promises. That's the other thing Liam and I always said. Or maybe it was left unsaid. Had I paid attention enough to know which? I started to like Nicole's attitude. She was more positive than I was. Maybe she was just the person to make me feel better right now. I decided to pick her brain a little.

"If you know so much, then where is he?" I asked her.

"I don't know."

"Thought you knew everything."

"Not everything. But I do know if he doesn't show, there's a good reason," Nicole replied gently.

"How can you be so sure?"

"You shared with him once, 'The strongest love story in classical literature is in the novel Wuthering Heights written by Emily Brontë where she develops the love story between Heathcliff and Catherine, proving the power of the emotion can carry on over a lifetime… The relationship begins with Heathcliff and Catherine meeting as children… The two hold a strong unbreakable connection, one that speaks without words. It is a love so solid, nothing could break it apart despite the unfavorable events placed upon them.'"

"So?" I said.

"Do you remember what he said?"

"Not exactly."

"He said, 'That's pretty solid,'" Nicole responded.

"So what?"

"So, he understands."

"He was quoting the quote. The quote says 'it is a love so solid.' He was quoting the quote, that's all."

"You don't think it meant anything to him?" she asked.

"I don't know."

"Didn't he say whatever was important to you, was important to him?"

"Stop!" I insisted. "I think—here's what I think. I think that what I think is irrelevant."

"That's not what you think, at all."

"But in the scheme of things, it's true. What I think really doesn't matter," I said.

"In the scheme of…?"

"Life, love, world hunger…"

Nicole sighed. "We were talking about Liam."

"And yes, Liam. What I think about Liam, what I feel about Liam—doesn't matter. I thought it was interesting that Heathcliff and Catherine met as children, just like Liam and I met as children. That's all."

"And how they never stopped loving each other even after they grew apart and married different people. Even had children with different people."

"Please, go away, now."

"Once you go through security, even if he makes it—" Nicole continued.

"He's not going to make it."

"But if he does, you'll already be at your gate and it will be too late and your heart is going to break."

"I'll be fine," I pounced.

"No, you won't."

Was she daring me? "Watch me."

"Empty threats."

"Whatever."

"If he doesn't make it, there will be a good reason," she said.

"Whatever you say," I decided.

"If you don't believe me, believe your heart," she whispered.

"My heart? My heart is what got me into this mess in the first place."

***

Instead of drowning in the disappointment I felt coming, I took a deep breath and let it wash over me like a tidal wave. Once fully immersed, I embraced the cleansing that water brings, and it miraculously held a portion of my sadness at bay. I yanked the handle of my carry-on up to its full position and directed my feet towards the *Passengers Only Beyond This Point* area.

Chapter Thirty-Five

In Your Eyes
Peter Gabriel, 1986

Several groups of people were beginning to congregate at the checkpoint in Santiago. Some were perusing maps, others were filling water containers, some were praying. Nicole's shoulders were already feeling the weight of her backpack when she became aware of a certain guy in the crowd. He looked somewhat familiar, most likely one of the passengers on the bus ride from the hotel, she thought. He was attractive, with a sense of calm self-assurance, but not the type who's comfortable calling attention to himself.

Nicole didn't know why she felt compelled to make eye contact with this person, but there was something drawing her to him. A discreet step in his direction brought her just close enough to make out his eyes behind his aviators. When they made eye contact, she felt her heart skip a beat the same way it had the very first time they met. She wanted to run to him but she was too overcome with emotion to move. She knew she should say something but she couldn't.

Garrett pulled a crumpled up, cotton bandana out of his jeans pocket and handed it to Nicole to wipe her tears. She took it from him graciously.

"Hi," he said.

"You decided to do this," she replied, dabbing her eyes.

"Ya."

"Good. Cuz, I mean, it's supposed to be good."

"So I hear."

"I have a map. At least, I did. Shoot, I think I left it on the bus. But you probably have one. If you don't, they'll probably have some at the next stop…" she rambled.

"I have a map," he said.

"Oh, good."

The silence that followed beckoned things that needed to be said, yet at the same time didn't seem necessary. Garrett looked at Nicole with the tender, steadfast gaze she knew so well. It was the look that removed all her defenses.

"All this time, I really did believe you hated me," Nicole said softly.

"Not possible," replied Garrett.

"It was wrong, what I did—" she said.

"It was beyond wrong."

"But, you're here. What about… what about your wife?"

"She went away for a while. To think, she said. I decided I could use some time to think, too."

"This is a long way to come just to think."

"I know. Every time I deal with you, I seem to change countries."

"Sorry."

"Don't worry about it."

"How have you been? It's been awful not knowing how you've been. It's nearly killed me—"

"We have a week to talk, Nicky. Let's wait a bit, eh?"

Garrett took Nicole's hand and they started down the dirt road, two kindred souls who found each other, then lost each other, and would find each other again. Just like always, with her hand in his, she felt grounded and safe and good and whole. And just like always, she quickened her pace to keep up with his.

Chapter Thirty-Six

All I Know
Art Garfunkel, 1973

"Ladies and gentlemen, at this time we ask that you please turn off all electronic devices including cell phones, or set them to 'airport mode' in order to disable internet access which could interfere with flight communication."

I checked my phone one last time. There was one new message: *Have a good flight, Mom! And don't be scared! Love, Sean.*

"Flight attendants, please prepare for takeoff."

It was the point in the flight where I always counted backwards from 10 to 1. But this time, I focused on the words from the reference to *Wuthering Heights*: 'The two hold a strong unbreakable connection, one that speaks without words. It is a love so solid, nothing could break it apart.'

The aircraft raced forward and shook with a deafening vibration. I was never sure which I hated more, take-off or landing. I squeezed my eyes shut and clenched my jaw and reminded myself this part would be over soon. I felt the nose of the Boeing lift up into the air, and waited for the loud roar to diminish to a soft hum.

Nicole's voice was gone from my head but she'd turned my focus to the love story I'd written. I thought of the chapter where she cried the entire flight home after finding Garrett with someone else. Right now, it made me want to cry, too, but I didn't. I thought of the chapter where she interrupted Garrett's wedding but the marriage took place anyway because despite our best efforts to control things, whatever's meant to be, will be. I thought of the chapter where she and Garrett sat under the tree in High Park and he took her hand in his, and placed it over his heart.

For the first time in decades, I found the courage to raise the window shade and look at the view outside the plane. I imagined writing *I love you* in a cloud formation across the sky, and wondered, if Liam looked up from wherever he was, would he see it.

A comment about the song titles:

One day while I was listening to one of my favorite songs, *'A Thousand Years'* by Sting, I discovered it embodied Miranda's belief that her love for Liam is timeless, and cannot be defined by the past, present or future. The hauntingly beautiful melody and lyrics of *'A Thousand Years'* reflects the core of Miranda's motivation to write her story. As I continued to write, I kept hearing other popular songs in my head that reflected what was going on with the characters, and eventually decided to use those songs as chapter titles. None of the choices were random, and though more than one recording artist may be famous for covering the song, the particular version indicated was purposefully chosen.

The Playlist

Take The Long Way Home, Supertramp

A Thousand Years, Sting

Traveling Boy, Art Garfunkel

Where Or When, Diana Krall

Truly, Lionel Richie

So Far Away, Carole King

Sorry Seems to Be the Hardest Word, Elton John

Every Breath You Take, The Police

Miss You, The Rolling Stones

Love In An Elevator, Aerosmith

Maybe I'm Amazed, Paul McCartney

(You Make Me Feel Like) A Natural Woman,
Aretha Franklin

Love You Inside Out, The Bee Gees

One Last Cry, Brian McKnight

Goin' Out of My Head, Queen Latifah

In Too Deep, Genesis

I Burn For You, Sting

She's Gone, Hall and Oates

Beautiful, Christina Aguilera

All I Do, Stevie Wonder

Wishing On a Star, Rose Royce

Smaointe, Enya

Will You Still Love Me, Chicago

Friends, Bette Midler

Hurt So Bad, Linda Rondstadt

Love Don't Live Here Anymore, Madonna

That's the Way I've Always Heard It Should Be,
Carly Simon

I Can't Make You Love Me, Bonnie Raitt

Sara Smile, Hall and Oates

Fly Away, Lenny Kravitz

Come Sail Away, Styx

Misunderstanding, Genesis

All I Want, Joni Mitchell

Listen to Your Heart, Roxette

In Your Eyes, Peter Gabriel

All I Know, Art Garfunkel

About the Author

Wanda Penalver Bevan was born and raised in Ithaca, New York. A graduate of Northwestern University, she's worked as an actress, paralegal, and events professional. She is the songwriter of *Little Girl* (2012), a tribute to the youngest victim of the 2011 Tucson shootings, and her poem, *America's Child* (1996), is on display at the Oklahoma City National Memorial. *Their Souls Met in Wishton* is her first fiction novel. Wanda lives in Phoenix, Arizona, following three decades in Southern California, whose ocean shores will always hold a piece of her heart.

Acknowledgements

There are many individuals to whom I owe gratitude.

First, to my parents, Marge and Ted, for encouraging me throughout my entire life and supporting me in whatever I pursued. They are my angels watching over me.

To my family and friends, for believing in me and standing by me through all the ups and downs that come with searching for one's creative voice. Your presence in my life is never taken for granted and your support means more than you know.

Erik Nance, Sheron McDonald, and Gary McLean, thank you for always being there to fuel my spirit. Without you I would never have been brave enough to write a book.

To Jill Cohen and Ashley Kravitz, for your suggestions that made significant improvements to the manuscript.

Thank you to the wonderful team at Solstice Publishing for everything!

To my editor, Brian Cavit, thank you for your guidance and patience.

Thank you to Kaaren Ragland who was the first person to hear my idea for a book and said "Write it."

There are some writers who deserve a special thanks. Diane Proctor Reeder, Jennifer M. Davies, Sue Fitzmaurice, B. Lynn Goodwin-Brown, Eric Vance Walton, Gina M. Angelone, Serita D. Stevens and Lana Short. You've each inspired me in a different way and make me feel honored to be a member of this terrifying, fulfilling, exhilaratingly insane club.

To Michael, thank you for your part in my life's journey.

To the amazing young women I am blessed to call my daughters, Amanda, Rosalind and Madison, it remains my greatest wish to be like you when I grow up. You remind me that there are miracles to be found everyday if we simply look for them and I love you more than any words in a book could describe.

Finally, to My Creator, I give thanks for the safety net I cannot see but is always there when I leap.

Social Media Links:

Blog:
https://wandaswayiswrite.wordpress.com

Instagram:
@wandaswayiswrite